SAY SOMETHING

Heather—
Thank you for stopping
by. It was a lot of
fun chatting!
♡
Beth H

ALSO BY BETH HILL

A Letter an Ex and Opal
Summer's Story

Say Something

Beth Hill

ISBNs: 978-1-7325424-0-2 (pb); 978-1-7325424-1-9 (Kindle); 978-1-7325424-2-6 (ePub)

Library of Congress Catalog Number: 2018907959
Printed in the United States of America
First Printing: 2018
22 21 20 19 18   5 4 3 2 1

Cover design and book design by Mayfly Design and typeset in the Whitman typeface

Good Vibes Publishing
To order, visit www.bethhill.com

For K, R and B –
May the light in you be all I see

SAY SOMETHING

1

OLIVE WOKE WITH A SMILE ON HER FACE. THE SUN WAS SHINING IN through her window, bright and clear, and the sky was blue. It was going to be a great day.

Glancing at the clock on her nightstand, she sent Simon a silent thank you for letting her sleep in. Some people would think rising at 8 am too early, but for Olive, it was pure gold. Her boys usually woke her by 6:30 am. Even though they were old enough to fend for themselves in the morning, most days she dragged herself out of bed and made them breakfast. The memory of oversleeping one morning and having to drop them off at school with only a handful of candy corn for breakfast was still fresh in her mind. She definitely didn't want to repeat that experience.

Slowly pushing back the covers of her bed, Olive took a moment to think of all she was grateful for, sending thanks out into the world. She then swung her legs over the side of her bed and stretched, standing up slowly and doing a few simple yoga poses. This little routine helped her feel ready for the day and let her wake up peacefully. If she could have fifteen minutes to do this each morning, she knew her day would be better for it.

After consciously inhaling and exhaling one last breath, Olive walked out of her room and down the hall towards the boys' rooms. She spent a couple of minutes making Beckett's bed and picking up his room. Then she grabbed the dirty clothes that were lying on the floor and tossed them out into the hallway. She did the same to Ben's room, and on the way out she grabbed the clothes on the hall floor and put them in the laundry machine, along with all the other laundry, and started a load.

She knew the boys could and should do these little chores themselves, and sometimes they did, but she liked doing it for them. Simon had been on her case, though, about how the boys needed more responsibility. She knew he was right; they did. They were growing up so fast though. One day they'd both be out of the house, living on their own, and she'd miss picking up their clothes and helping clean their rooms. So she did a little extra now, hoping she wouldn't miss it so much then.

As she walked down the stairs she smelled bacon, and her stomach growled. She saw Simon, Ben, and Beckett all scurrying around the kitchen, and her heart filled with happiness. Beckett was setting out plates, napkins, and silverware, Ben was pulling out hot sauce and ketchup from the fridge, and Simon was lifting the eggs out of the pan and into a bowl.

Setting the bowl down beside a plate of bacon and a huge stack of pancakes, Simon looked up at Olive and smiled. "There she is," he said, walking over to give her a quick kiss.

"Yuck! Seriously, you guys!" Ben remarked, disgusted, as Beckett made kissing noises.

Olive laughed, knowing it was only half true. She could see how happy he was that they, Olive and Simon, were happy, that they loved each other.

She took a seat between Ben and Beckett, and watched Simon load up the plates. He caught her watching him and winked at her, and her heart skipped a beat. She was sometimes surprised at how in love with him she was. At how strong their connection was, still, after all the years they'd been together. She had thought that, over time, things would settle a little, become more comfortable and relaxed, lukewarm. But they hadn't, not in the least. She was more in love with him now than when they'd been first married, and she felt lucky that they hadn't lost that.

After all plates were loaded up, Simon grabbed the syrup from the sink, where it sat in a bowl of hot water, and wiped it off. Olive always laughed at Simon because he would never put their syrup, which was in a microwavable bottle, in the microwave. He refused to use the microwave unless it was absolutely necessary, stating it was unhealthy and unethical to put out 'toxic waves' if you didn't need to. Olive, on the other hand, loved the microwave and used it enough for the both of them.

Opening the syrup, Simon leaned forward and drizzled some across Beckett's pancakes, and then Ben's. If left to the boys, they would use the entire bottle and still grumble that there wasn't enough.

"So," he said as he loaded up his own pancakes with more than enough syrup, "what's on the docket today? The boys and I are thinking about checking out that new outdoors store that's just opened up down the road and then heading over to the lake to do some fishing."

"Mmm," Olive responded, nodding and chewing a bite of bacon, "That sounds fun. I'm not quite sure what my plans are yet, but I was thinking about checking out the new bike paths across from the school. I read in the paper they've added some new trails, and I thought it'd be fun to check them out. Oh, and don't forget Gizzy is coming this weekend too"—Olive paused to laugh as the boys cheered—"She misses you, says she hasn't seen enough of you lately."

Beckett frowned and responded, "That's because we've been at school. I'd rather be at Gizzy's."

Ben nodded, looking glum, and agreed, "Me too. It's only been like two weeks since school started, but it feels like a million years."

"I know. Barf," Beckett added, cracking up at the look Olive gave him.

Gizzy was Olive's mom, whose actual name was Mara. When Ben was a little over a year old and had started to say a few words, one of his first was 'gizzy.' Olive and Simon had no idea what he was saying. "What in the world could 'gizzy' mean?" they wondered. Maybe they were hearing it wrong? But no, he would look out the window and say, "Gizzy, gizzy, gizzy," over and over and over.

About a week into his gizzy phase, Mara came over to watch Ben, so Olive and Simon could have a date night. When Mara walked in the door, Ben went crazy, shouting, "Gizzy! Gizzy! Gizzy!"

"What's that about?" Mara asked, as Olive and Simon looked at each other and burst out laughing.

"We've been trying to figure out all week what 'gizzy' means," Olive explained, between bursts of laughter, "and we've just figured it out. He's saying, 'Grandma'! You're Gizzy!"

"Gizzy, huh?" Mara said as she picked up Ben and snuggled him, "For you, my sweetheart, I'll be whatever you want."

From then on Mara was known as Gizzy, and even though it wasn't the prettiest name a grandma could have, she loved it because it was a Ben original.

"Then," Olive added, "when you guys get home, I can tell you about the trails. If I'm not too exhausted, maybe we can ride them as a family tonight." She took a big bite of pancakes and closed her eyes, savoring the flavor. Simon was the best cook.

"Yeah!" Beckett cried, "Oh, and can we get ice cream when Gizzy gets here?"

"Please Mom! But first I want to show her my new house I made on Minecraft," Ben said, his mouth full of food.

Olive shrugged, stating, "If it's fine with Gizzy, it's fine with me."

Olive's mom lived about an hour away in the house Olive had grown up in. Olive sometimes worried that the upkeep of an old house like that would be too much for her mom, but Mara had insisted time and again that she had no plans of moving out anytime soon. The house was special to her, and she enjoyed tinkering around, making sure it stayed in tip-top shape.

Olive was looking forward to her mother's visit. Even though Olive was a grown woman, at thirty-five years old she still sometimes longed for her mother, at times wishing she lived right next door. She enjoyed the time they had together and always felt a little blue when her mom left to go back home.

Simon was slightly mystified by Olive's close relationship with her mother. He had lost both of his parents in a car accident when he was in his second year of college. He'd never had a particularly close relationship with either his mother or father, but he'd always longed for what he considered to be a true family. That was what Olive loved about him from right off the bat, his unabashed longing for a family. For kids. For a relationship that meant something. She always felt that she had struck gold when she met Simon.

"Well, boys," Simon announced, picking up his empty plate and walking it over to the dishwasher, "finish up and we'll head out. I'm planning on catching the biggest fish you've ever seen." He winked at them as he put his hands on Olive's shoulders and rubbed.

"No way!" Beckett cried, shoveling in the rest of his eggs, "I'm going to catch it!"

"Sorry, but it's going to be me, man. I just have a feeling," Ben interjected, elbowing Beckett as he stood up and went to clear his plate.

Beckett lunged forward, sticking his tongue out at Ben and nearly knocking over his milk.

"Boys, boys!" Simon declared, clapping his hands, "Get upstairs and get dressed before I leave without you." He smiled at them as they raced up the stairs, their sticky hands grabbing onto the railing as they threw out bets on who'd win. "And wash your hands!" Simon called up after them.

Olive leaned back, relaxing into the massage. "Thanks for breakfast and for taking the boys today. It'll be nice to have a few hours to myself," she told him with a smile.

"Of course," he replied as he leaned down to kiss her, "You deserve it. Do you need some help loading your bike into the car?"

Olive's heart warmed, he was so good to her. "No, but thank you. I think I'm going to head out from here. Go have fun with those monsters," she said, smiling as she heard feet running and jumping, "They're sure excited."

"So am I," Simon added, pulling her off her bar stool and into a hug. "I'm going to catch the fish and win the bet," he remarked with a smile as he brushed a hair out of her eye and kissed her again, then turned to start loading the dishwasher.

"No, no, I got this," Olive insisted, taking the glass out of his hand, "Get out of here." She smiled and nudged him away playfully. She was going to miss him and the boys. It was silly, she knew. They were only going to be away for a few hours at the most. Still, whenever they were apart, it was as if a piece of her were missing. She was never quite herself unless her family was altogether.

She watched her boys race down the stairs together, laughing, and she was filled with so much joy it almost hurt. This was what she loved, these little moments that could escape you if you weren't paying attention.

"Bye, Mom! Bye!" they called out in unison as they careened past her through the kitchen and into the mudroom to find their tennis shoes.

"Bye, boys. Love you!" she responded as she leaned in for one last hug from Simon. "See you soon," she said happily and gave him a quick kiss on the cheek. "And good luck," she added as the boys slammed shut the door to the garage, applying so much force it practically shook the entire house.

Simon winked at her as he grabbed his phone and hurried out the door.

After loading the dishwasher and wiping down the countertops, Olive went upstairs to change. Figuring she'd have enough time to take a shower after her bike ride, she pulled on her favorite black yoga pants and a black tank.

Walking back downstairs, she pulled her short strawberry blonde hair into a low ponytail and laughed. At the very top edge of one of their big living room windows she spotted two Nerf darts. The boys must have been having a battle this morning while Simon cooked breakfast. Olive knew those darts would drive some moms crazy, but not her. She loved seeing little signs of her kids around the house—the darts stuck in weird places, the Lego guys set up in imaginary combat, prized drawings taped or sometimes stapled to their walls ("No staples, boys! Please, no staples!" Simon would always exclaim). Except for the fingerprints on the windows, that was the one thing that drove her crazy, but she tried not to let it bother her too much. She knew one day she just might miss it.

Olive walked into the kitchen and double-checked that Simon had turned off the burner. He sometimes forgot and left it on though he would never admit it. Once she came home and was about to turn on the stove to make dinner when she noticed it was already on. Puzzled, she wracked her brain trying to remember the last time she had used the stove. She wasn't much of a cook, and she remembered that Simon had been making something that morning. The burner had, in fact, been on all day long.

Thankfully the house hadn't burnt down, and Olive had one more thing to add to her checklist each morning: check burner, always check burner.

He had remembered this time, so Olive gave him a mental high-five as she slid her shoes on and walked into the garage. As she grabbed her bike, she had a fleeting thought of skipping the ride entirely and staying home instead. She could take a long steamy shower, make some tea, and maybe dive into one of the books on her nightstand. But no. She had been wanting to check out the new bike trails for a while now, and she knew she'd feel better getting some exercise than she would sitting around doing nothing.

So, she grabbed her bike and hopped on, popping in her earbuds.

Rolling down the driveway, Olive took a deep breath of fresh air. She smiled, trying to shake off an odd sensation that felt like dread. Stopping her bike, Olive frowned and pulled her earbuds out. Stashing them in the tiny zippered pocket on the hip of her yoga pants, she wondered what her deal was. Maybe she just missed her family? Maybe Simon had used expired milk when he'd mixed up the pancake batter, and it was making her feel off?

Looking up at the blue, cloudless sky and feeling the sunshine on her face, Olive told herself she was just being silly. She told herself whatever this feeling was, it was probably nothing. It would probably be gone by the time she got home from her bike ride. She'd probably have forgotten all about it.

Olive made her way down the sidewalk and through her neighborhood, waving at neighbors as she passed. She called out a quick hello to Tucker, one of Ben's friends from down the street, who was shooting hoops with his younger brother.

She thought about Ben as she peddled along, proud of all he had accomplished this year in school, despite all of his struggles. Ben had been diagnosed with dyslexia a year and a half ago, and since that diagnosis, things at school had been slowly but surely getting better. He had finally been able to get the help that he needed with reading, math, and writing, and for the first time in his school career, Olive felt hopeful.

Before his diagnosis, things had been rough. Ben had hated school, he had said over and over to her and Simon that he was stupid, a dummy. Those words spewing out of her beautiful son's mouth had ripped her to shreds, leaving her feeling confused and afraid. She knew Ben was smart. She had seen him take apart almost anything he could get his hands on and put it back together again faster than even she could manage to do. She had heard him explain many times the inner workings of what it was he had taken apart; he always knew exactly how things fit together, what made them work.

She had always been amazed at his mind, how it could pick up minute details and turn them into something else entirely. When had she ever looked at the airplane ride at the fair and thought about how exactly its parts fit together to make the airplanes move up and down? Never, until Ben had pointed it out to her, explaining how the entire process worked.

He was fun and sweet and, in her eyes, brilliant, but he was also a little different than other kids his age. When he started school, it became glaringly obvious that something wasn't right. From the first day of kindergarten, when his anxiety went through the roof and continued on through second grade, when he still hadn't caught up with his peers, Olive knew something was going on that they couldn't quite figure out.

Finally, after much testing and waiting and filling out of questionnaires, they had an answer—dyslexia. Neither Olive nor Simon knew much about it, but having an answer to what had been crushing their son was a huge relief. They didn't want to label their son, they never would, but having something to bring back to the school, something that could get Ben the help he needed, was an answer to their prayers.

Olive literally had felt a weight lift off her shoulders when she'd heard from the school that Ben would be able to get all the help he needed. Because the school could only do so much testing, and the testing they'd had done hadn't shown enough need for him to get extra help, Olive and Simon had gone elsewhere for more in-depth tests. It had been stressful and sad and expensive, and sometimes Olive had felt like everyone was just looking for what was wrong with Ben, but in the end, it had been worth it, only because Ben had gotten what he required, and that was what mattered most to Olive.

So things had been going well this year, and even though Olive knew Ben would have some struggles ahead of him, she knew he would make it. He was a hard worker, determined to do what he had to do, and she was so very proud of him.

She was hopeful that his progress would be obvious at his IEP meeting this year, but that was still about six months away. Olive knew the best thing was to stay optimistic and just be there for Ben, making sure he was getting what he needed.

Olive pulled herself out of her thoughts and back into the present. Because she wanted to enjoy this time she had to herself, she reminded herself that there would be plenty of time to think about all the other things she needed to do, but now she should just enjoy the moment.

And that's when it happened. As Olive gave her bike a big push forward, out onto the street, she glanced down quickly at her phone to make sure it was secured in its holder. There was a loud screeching, followed by an even louder honking. It was at that moment, as Olive was flying through the air in what seemed to her to be slow motion, that she thought, *And this is why I always tell my kids to pay attention,* followed by, *That's why I was feeling so weird a second ago,* followed by, *Oh crap.*

* * *

Whatever they had done to cure the pain, it had worked. Olive woke up blissfully relaxed, feeling lighter, better than she had felt in forever. But when she opened her eyes and looked around, she was confused. She could see her body lying on a hospital bed, surrounded by doctors and nurses. It looked like they were trying to revive her with those metal pad things that send out electric shocks.

She started to panic. *What's going on?* she tried to shout, but her voice wouldn't work. She tried again. Nothing. She was about to try for a third time when she suddenly felt warm, fuzzy, and extremely relaxed. She gave into the feeling and drifted off to sleep.

* * *

Opening her eyes, she tried shouting out a *Hello, where am I?* but there was nothing. Feeling afraid, she closed her eyes. There was something there … but what?

She could feel Him before she could see Him. Something big and warm and beautiful that brought tears to her eyes and filled her with complete love. It was a feeling bigger than anything she could remember feeling before. She had to close her eyes, so it was easier to take in.

"Hello, Olive," He said. Or did He? It was more of a thought that she could hear than a spoken word.

"Hello," she replied, startling herself. She had no idea how she'd done it, that talking but not talking thing. She heard Him laugh.

"I love you," He said, "I'll see you soon." And then He was gone.

"Wait!" she cried out. She was confused, she wanted to know what was going on. If that was … HIM, like really HIM, then wouldn't that mean she was … ? But no. She couldn't be … dead, could she? She started to cry.

* * *

Feeling someone calling her name, she quieted her crying and looked around. At first there was nothing though she knew someone had been calling her. She heard it again, and then there he was. Not Him, but someone else.

She could tell it was someone different because of how he felt. This one didn't feel as bright, but he still felt shiny, and he made her feel really, really happy.

It was weird because she couldn't really see, but she had a vision of what he looked like, and it was almost like an angel. She started crying again, afraid of what this meant. This not being able to see, but still see. This not being able to speak, but still speak.

He smiled at her thought, and her fears vanished and her vision cleared. He had a beautiful smile that radiated love and happiness.

"Hello," he said, "I'm Michael."

"Michael?" she replied, "I'm so confused. Why am I here? What is this place? I want to go back to my family."

"Olive," he began, "you've had an accident. Do you remember?"

She shook her head, answering, "No." She then declared more loudly, "No!"

"Olive, you are in Heaven now. I'm here to help you."

"No!" she screamed, "This wasn't supposed to happen! I'm not supposed to be here!"

"Olive," he said again, "Olive, look at me. Everything happens for a reason, but I promise it's going to be okay."

Taking a deep breath, she looked up at him, into his eyes, and felt a kind of understanding. She knew he was being honest, she could believe him, trust him. But she didn't want to. She wouldn't believe that it was meant to be this way, getting ripped away from her family. No, she wasn't going to accept it.

"Come with me," he told her. "There is something you need to see, but you're going to have to trust me. This isn't going to be easy."

She looked at him, confused, as he pulled her through.

2

"Where are we?" she asked. "What's going on?" She thought she should be afraid, but being with Michael gave her peace.

"I told you before, this is going to be hard, but it's something you need to see. You have to trust me, Olive. I will keep you safe, and I promise everything is going to be okay."

"Where are we?" she asked quietly, even though she was pretty sure of his answer.

"We are at the hospital, Olive. We are going with the doctor when he tells your husband you didn't make it." He stretched his hand towards hers, offering, "Here, take my hand."

Grabbing his hand, she felt more peace flowing through her, but it didn't erase the sadness.

Spotting a tired-looking doctor in light-blue scrubs, Michael looked down at her with love and asked, "You ready?"

"What choice do I have?" Olive replied, as they followed the doctor around the corner to where her husband sat. Head in hands.

"Mr. Walker?" the doctor said quietly.

Simon's head snapped up, and Olive was grateful that there were no other people in the waiting room. At least he'd have privacy, if only for a moment.

"Yes," Simon answered, standing up quickly. His eyes searching the doctor's for any clues.

Placing a hand on Simon's shoulder, the doctor spoke, "I'm so sorry, Mr. Walker, but she didn't make it. There was nothing we could do. I'm so sorry."

For a moment, a few seconds, Simon stood there, staring at the doctor as if he hadn't quite heard, and Olive wished she could do something. Wished she could pop out from where she was and shout, "Just kidding! Here I am!"

But then that moment passed, and Simon collapsed back into the chair he had been sitting in and broke down.

Olive was broken-hearted. She wanted to hug him, kiss him, hold his hand—do something to make him feel better—but she couldn't.

Feeling Michael beside her, she looked up at him.

"It's going to be okay," he assured and nodded towards the doctor.

Olive turned her attention back to her husband and saw that the doctor had kneeled down beside him and was hugging him, patting his back. The doctor sat back on his heels and disclosed, "It's going to be tough for a while, Simon, I won't lie. But I promise you, things will be okay. You will be okay and so will your boys."

Looking up at the doctor with red, wet eyes, Simon sobbed. "The boys!" he cried, "What am I supposed to tell the boys?"

Swallowing the lump in his throat, the doctor replied, "The truth. Just tell them the truth."

If Olive's heart hadn't been broken before, it was now. She thought she could actually feel it cracking in half, breaking into a million tiny pieces, never to be the same again. Her boys. Her sweet, lovely, wild boys. What was she going to do without them? Her death was going to crush them. They had absolutely no idea what was coming. They were going to be blindsided, and it was all her fault.

She couldn't take it anymore. It wasn't fair. *This* wasn't fair. Watching the doctor give Simon a final hug and then walk away, she broke down. "Simon!" she screamed, "I'm right here!"

Simon slowly got up and started walking towards the exit, towards home.

"Simon!" she continued to scream—he was right beside her now, so why couldn't he hear her?—"Simon! I'm here, I'm right here!" She reached out to grab him, but he walked right through her.

She felt Michael beside her. "Olive," he voiced.

"No!" she cried, pushing away from him, "There's been a mistake! Take me back! Take me back to my body and make me wake up, let me go back to my family. Please! Please!" she begged, her voice ragged.

Michael was beside her again. "Olive," he spoke, touching her shoulder to calm her down, "what happened was meant to happen. I know you don't understand that now, but you will. I'm sorry you're hurting, but there is nothing we can do to change it."

Olive looked up at Michael. She knew what he was saying was true, but she wasn't ready to accept it. Not yet.

"I love you, Olive," he told her, and she felt it. She felt his pure, unconditional love, and she felt something else too, but she wasn't sure what it was. She'd find out later though that that feeling was her spirit slowly, very slowly starting to heal.

"Come on," he instructed, taking her hand, "There is something else we need to do. This is going to be the hardest thing for you on your journey, but I believe in you. I'm here for you, Olive. It's going to be okay."

He pulled her through again.

* * *

They were at her house. She saw her mom's car parked in the driveway and felt sick all over again. Michael touched her shoulder and gave her peace.

They followed Simon inside. Olive wondered why watching him made her feel like she was watching a movie; it didn't feel real. She didn't feel as connected to him and to what was about to happen as she thought she should.

"Some things are too much to feel at once, Olive, but you still need to see it, feel some of it. This is one way I can help you. I can take some of the hurt away until you are ready to feel it all. When you are ready, when you fully accept what has happened, then you have the choice to go back and feel it all. Experience it completely. I want you to feel safe, Olive," Michael gently explained.

She watched Simon open the door, heard what he heard: the sounds of her boys. They were playing Mario Kart, laughing, screaming gleefully. The sounds filled her with joy and extreme pain at the same time. Michael gave her peace.

Simon quietly shut the door, kicked off his shoes, and slowly walked through the mudroom and into the kitchen, where Olive's mom, Mara, was sitting at the table, mindlessly flicking through *Parents* magazine. Upon seeing Simon enter the kitchen, Mara stood up abruptly, causing the chair she had been sitting in to teeter backwards and almost topple over. She put her hand on the chair to steady it—and herself—as she asked, "How is she?"

Olive heard the hope in her mom's voice. She could feel how much her mom loved her, feel how much her mom just wanted to make things better.

Time seemed to stop. Olive just wanted to get away from here, run as far and as fast as she could. When she felt Michael beside her, she felt braver and more at peace, but she still felt sad.

"How is she?" her mother asked again.

Simon just shook his head.

He shook his head and tried to hold back his sobs. Mara ran to hug him and the magazine fluttered to the floor. They stood there for a while, rocking back and forth in each other's arms, crying, too much in shock to say anything.

Olive looked away. She didn't want to see this, their hurt over her.

"Olive," Michael explained, "what happens next is going to be the absolute hardest part. This is going to be the most difficult thing you go through, but I need you to trust me. I am here for you. You need to know and believe that everything will be okay. You need to be brave and strong. You need to do this for your boys. If you can do this, I promise that things will start to get easier, but you need to trust me, Olive. Fight through this, fight for your boys."

"I don't understand," Olive divulged.

"It's time," Michael stated, at the same time as Simon said, "I need to tell the boys."

Mara nodded. "Would you like me to give you some privacy?" she asked.

"No, please," Simon answered, gesturing towards the couch where the boys were sitting with their Wii controllers, "I don't think I can do this alone."

Mara nodded again and took his hand as they both walked into the living room.

"Ah, Dad!" cried Ben, as Simon walked in front of the boys and sat down beside Ben on the couch. Mara slowly sat down on the loveseat. "You totally blocked my view, and now I crashed!" complained Ben, slumping against the back of the couch with a defeated look on his face.

"Vic-to-ry! Vic-to-ry!" Beckett chanted, jumping up and dancing around the room with his hands in the air.

This made Olive smile, but her eyes stung with tears and her heart felt heavy. Michael touched her shoulder, and she felt a little bit lighter.

"Boys," Simon started, his voice cracking. He cleared his throat and tried again, "Boys, Gizzy and I have something we need to talk to you about. Please sit down."

Sitting straight up, Ben quickly offered, "I swear, Dad, I swear! I didn't hit him first, he hit me! I didn't start the fight, I ended it, like you said I could, Dad!" Ben looked at Simon nervously, waiting to see what his fate would be.

Beckett jumped backwards onto the couch, landing next to Ben, and laughed.

Mara chuckled softly. "No, boys, it's nothing to do with that," she assured them as she stood up and walked over to turn off the Wii. The boys groaned.

Tears started streaming down Olive's face. She knew why her mom had turned off the Wii. Mario Kart was the boys' favorite game, and she didn't want it to be ruined for them. She didn't want them to never enjoy it again because it reminded them of her death.

Her mom must have thought of that too or sensed what Olive was thinking. "Thank you, Mom," Olive whispered, and at that moment, Mara stopped in her tracks on the way to the loveseat and glanced around the room. Shaking her head, she took the last few steps toward the loveseat next to the couch and sat down.

"Did she just hear me?" Olive asked, shocked.

She felt warmth, Michael was smiling, and she had a fleeting feeling of everything being okay.

"Boys, what we have to talk about is Mom," Simon slowly began, unsure of how to proceed. He got up off the couch and kneeled down in front of them, looking up into their eyes.

"What about Mom?" Ben asked accusingly.

"Yeah, where's Mom? She promised she'd play Mario with us, she was going to be Baby Peach!" Beckett added, looking at his father expectantly.

Simon took a deep breath and continued, "Boys, your mom had an accident today and had to be taken to the hospital."

"What accident?" cried Ben, alarmed.

"Where's Mommy, Daddy?" asked Beckett, his eyes wide, full of worry.

Olive couldn't breathe for a moment, she couldn't move. She was paralyzed with anger. She hated this. She hated what had happened, and she hated herself for putting her family through this. She started to pull herself away, from Michael and from what she was seeing play out in front of her.

"Olive, remember what I told you: this is going to be hard, getting through this will be the hardest thing you've ever done, but you can do it.

Trust me," Michael reminded her. He gave her peace, but she didn't want it, she was angry.

"Daddy?" cried Beckett.

"Simon," Mara said quietly, wanting him to ease their fears, but knowing he couldn't.

"Daddy!" Ben barked.

"Olive," Michael stated as she tried to pull away.

She was shaking now, in anger and heartbreak and regret. She wanted to rip herself away from this: from having to see her boys hurting, her husband trying to be strong but dying inside, her mom losing her baby.

"No!" she screamed, "I will not do this! I will not watch this! What difference does it make? I'm gone, I'm dead! Why do I need to see this? What good does it do me? All it does is hurt, it hurts so much, and I'm not strong enough for this. I just . . . can't."

"Olive, trust me. Stay here with me, Olive. I know you don't understand this now, but you need this to heal. You need this to help your family heal. Your boys need you, Olive. Your husband needs you, your mom. If you want to help them, if you want them to have peace, you need to stay with me here. You need to fight your way through this."

He looked at her, and she could feel how much he loved her. She could feel his pain in regard to her hurting. She could feel how much he loved her boys. She saw that he was pouring blessings down onto them as they sat on the couch. It looked like sparkling, golden pixie dust falling onto them, floating and spinning and making them glow. She blinked and looked again, noticing that it was on Simon now too, and her mom.

She took a breath and felt Michael's peace in her heart. She took the biggest breath she could and imagined the peace he was giving her filling up her entire body and making her whole, keeping her brave. She felt her tears flowing, but she didn't look away.

"Brave," she heard him say, "You are being so very brave."

"Ben, Beckett," Simon began, taking their small hands in his bigger ones, "I love you so much. I love you so much that I can't even measure it, I can't even put into words how much. Maybe one day when you are both daddies, then you will understand."

"Dad?" Ben asked quietly.

"I'm so sorry to have to tell you this," Simon said and paused to clear his throat.

Olive's heart was thudding, breaking, burning, crying. All she wanted to do was take her boys in her arms and hold them as tightly as she could, but she couldn't.

Michael gave her peace. He held her hand, he calmed her heart.

"I'm so sorry, boys, but Mommy . . . Mommy died today. I'm so sorry . . ." Simon managed to articulate before a sob escaped his lips.

"No!" Ben retorted, "No! Mom can't die, she isn't dead. No, Dad. No!" He fell into Simon's lap crying at the same time as Beckett started to scream.

"Moooommmmmyyyyy! Mommy, come back! Moooommm!" screeched Beckett over and over and over, as Mara held him in her lap and rocked him back and forth, weeping her own tears.

Olive felt Michael. She felt him put his arms around her. She felt him put something over her ears to muffle the sounds. She was trying to get to her boys, to hold her boys, to make it better, but she couldn't. No matter what she did, she just couldn't get to them.

She started to scream. She started to fight. And then she was gone.

* * *

"You did a good job, Olive," He said, "I know that was extremely hard for you, but you did well." He hugged her.

"Thank you," she replied, then added, "I didn't want to leave them."

She felt Him smile, felt His love flowing over her. "I know," He shared, "I am so proud at how much you love them. It's so beautiful to see. You are a lovely example of what a mother's love is like."

She was somewhere big and warm and light. Somewhere vast and open, beautiful. It startled her how different things were, but there was something achingly familiar about it also.

"Why?" she asked. "Why did you take me? Why did I have to go?" She was calm now. She always was calm around Him. She was happy, but still sad, and she longed for her family, her boys especially.

She felt His love, felt how He wanted to ease her pain. She could feel how He longed to take her sorrow on Himself, but couldn't, because this was her lesson.

"This is hard to understand now, Olive, but what happened was meant to happen. One day, when you are healed and the pain has passed, you will understand why you were meant to come here now."

Her heart hurt, and she felt Him take some of her pain away anyway, even though it was hers alone. It reminded her of how when her boys were sick or hurting, she would wish she could take their pain and deal with it herself, so that they wouldn't have to suffer.

She felt Him laugh, knowing her thoughts.

"That's exactly it, Olive. I love you, and I don't want to see you hurting, so I do what I can to help you. But"—He paused—"what good would it do if I took away all your pain? You need to feel some to grow, to learn, and to be able to heal yourself. That's the only way you'll accept what happened and move on to do even greater things."

"What if I don't want to do greater things? What if all I want is to go back to my family?" she asked.

He looked at her, straight into her eyes, and she felt warm and fuzzy and full of light. She felt so completely loved that it took her breath away, and she started to cry because it was all too much.

"I'm afraid that's impossible, Olive," He stated.

"It's not impossible! Nothing's impossible!" she cried, feeling scared and unsure, but feeling Him and His love still.

He laughed, delighted at her thoughts. "That's true," He replied.

"I want to go home!" she cried, "I want to see my family! I want to make sure my boys are okay, Simon and my mom, too! I need to be there for Ben, he needs me the most. I can't just *leave* him!" She was sobbing now. She could feel Him near her, she could feel His love. Wiping her eyes, she looked up at Him, as best she could, steadied her voice, and begged, "I'll do anything to go back. I will do anything."

"I'm giving you some time to heal now, Olive. Michael will be with you to show you the way. Oh, and Olive," He said with gravity, "you need to know that the harder it is for you to accept what has happened, the harder it is for your family. I know you love them and think that accepting this means letting them go or giving up on them, but that's not true. In time you'll come to understand that your moving on from where you are helps them move on from where they are." Then He smiled and said, "Remember, Olive, I love you," and He was gone.

3

IT HAD BEEN OVER TWO WEEKS, AND THE BOYS WERE STILL INCONSOL-
able. Ben wouldn't come out of his room unless forced, and when he did, his
eyes were red and puffy. Simon remembered all the talks he had given Ben in
years past, about how boys were brave and didn't cry. How they had to buck
up when they were hurt. Those words were killing him now. He wished he
could go back and erase every single one. He had thought he had been prepar-
ing Ben to be a man, but now he wasn't so sure. How could you prepare a boy
to lose his mother? You couldn't. How could you undo words since passed?
He didn't think you could do that either.

He wanted Ben to be able to come to him and tell him how he felt, talk to
him. He wanted him to open up and let it all out, so that they could begin to
heal together. Unfortunately, that wasn't happening. Ben clammed up when Simon was around, answering all of Simon's questions with either a yes or no, if
he could get away with it. When Simon demanded more of an answer, Ben used
as few words as possible and then snuck upstairs when Simon wasn't looking.

Beckett was another story. He wouldn't let Simon out of his sight. He ate,
slept, and breathed Simon. If Simon left the room without Beckett, he would
completely melt down, screaming and shrieking until Simon came back. Simon couldn't do anything without Beckett, not even go to the bathroom. Simon had no idea how he was going to manage going back to work and getting
the boys back to school.

His only saving grace was Mara. The boys absolutely adored her. When
she was there, which was beginning to be around-the-clock, the boys would
let go a little bit. Ben would come out of his room and hang out with the family. At bedtime, Ben and Mara would sit on Ben's bed and talk quietly, sometimes late into the night. Simon was glad Ben was opening up to someone
even though he wished it were to him. Simon thought he even heard Ben
laugh once last night.

When Mara was around, Beckett would actually let Simon leave the room for a couple of minutes, as long as he knew where Simon was going and that he would most definitely be back. Simon was now free to go to the bathroom alone and throw together a quick lunch or dinner. "Thank you," he had said more times than he could count to Mara. "I don't know what I'd do if you weren't here," he'd add.

Mara would just wave her hand and say, "Please," and give a small smile, or "There's nowhere else I'd rather be." And he believed her. He knew the best place to be when you missed someone you love is with family. With the people that know you best, knew the person you miss best.

He was half thinking of asking her to stay with them, but he wasn't sure if that would be asking too much. It wasn't her responsibility to take care of two grieving kids and their hopeless father, but he felt like maybe she needed them as much as they needed her. Or maybe that was just his own wishful thinking. Sure, she lived only an hour away, but knowing she'd be there whenever they needed her gave him comfort.

Creeping out of Beckett's bedroom, Simon felt his phone vibrating. He quickly and quietly hurried through the hall and down the stairs before he answered with a hushed, "Hello?" He recognized it was the school calling and knew he couldn't avoid their calls much longer. The boys had already missed a couple of weeks of school, and he didn't think he was going to get them there anytime soon.

"Hello? Mr. Walker? This is Jo Thorne, the school counselor. Is now a good time to talk?"

Jo Thorne, the name rang a bell. He was pretty sure she had left a couple of messages already. "Yes, this is Simon. Sure, now is an okay time," he agreed reluctantly, sitting down on the couch, hoping he wouldn't get an earful for letting his boys skip school and not returning her calls.

"Good," she replied, cleared her throat, and continued, "I know this has been a hard time for you and your family, Mr. Walker."

"Yes," he confirmed, "it's been tough, to say the least." He swallowed hard and tried not to think of Olive. He didn't want to get choked up, but it was impossible not to. He'd been trying to hold it together for the boys, and it helped if he just focused on them. But at night, when they were asleep and everything was quiet and he was lying in an empty bed ... those were the times when his grief was the strongest.

"I'm calling, Mr. Walker, to see if there is anything I can do for you or your boys. I know they've been out of school for two weeks, and that's to be expected, but it's important that they get back to their normal routine, their normal schedule," she told him, then added, "I don't want to seem pushy, Mr. Walker. I understand how this is. I just think . . . I think that getting back to our daily lives and pushing ourselves to keep going, even though it seems like the hardest thing in the world, is what starts the healing process."

Simon was still holding back tears. He knew the day would come when he'd have to face the reality of a normal life without Olive, which in itself seemed contradictory—how could life be normal without Olive? He just didn't think that day would be now. He thought of his boys, having to go back to how things were before, when their little hearts were breaking.

He responded, "Yes, well, one of them won't come out of his room, and the other can't stand to be away from me at all. Ever. So, I'm having a hard time wrapping my mind around how I'm going to get them back to school." Feeling like a jerk, he added, "Don't get me wrong, Ms. Thorne. I do agree that they need to get back into the swing of things. It just seems a little early, is all."

She laughed quietly and remarked, "Let me guess. Ben won't come out of his room, and Beckett is now your bathroom buddy?"

This made him laugh a little, the first time since Olive, and he was surprised. "Yes, spot-on," he admitted, then felt guilty for laughing.

She seemed to sense it because she said, "Finding a little humor in the midst of heartbreak is sometimes just what we need"—she paused—"Anyway, would you be open to me talking to the boys? I'd like to get a sense of how they are doing, where they are at with what has all happened. It would help me get a good idea of the best way to ease them back into their everyday life." She waited for him to reply, and when he didn't right away, she added, "I hope I'm not over stepping my bounds, Mr. Walker. It's just that . . . I've gotten to know Ben and Beckett from seeing them in the halls and the classroom, at lunch and recess. They honestly are two of the sweetest boys, and it hurts me to know that they are hurting. I just want to do whatever I can to help."

Simon wasn't sure what to say. He closed his eyes and tried to think. He didn't know this Jo lady, and he wasn't sure if Olive had known her or what she'd thought of her. Olive was the school person of their family. She'd taken the boys to get their supplies, she'd taken them to back-to-school night, and she'd scheduled their conferences, usually attending alone with Simon at home with the boys. She'd volunteered and gone on as many field trips as possible. It had been something that she'd loved to do, so it hadn't bothered her that Simon had been more in the background in that department.

Now though, he wished he had been more in tune with all things school. How would he know which teachers were the best for the boys? Especially Ben, because he was more sensitive and had more stuff going on than Beckett. How would he know what the boys usually took for snack, or what their favorite water bottles were? How would he know when they wanted cold lunch instead of hot, or what they liked in their lunch? Didn't Olive say she sometimes snuck a couple of Oreos into their lunchboxes? Or were the Oreos the special snack they only got on Wednesdays after they had finished their homework, and only if she had gotten a good midweek update from the teacher? Did teachers even send midweek updates? What time did school start? What time did it end? He was so confused. He closed his eyes, rubbing his forehead.

"Mr. Walker?" Jo's voice echoed out of the phone.

"Honestly," he confessed, overwhelmed, "I have no idea if I'd be okay with that. Olive did all of the school stuff, and I don't remember her mentioning you. What if she didn't like you? What if she hated you? I most definitely couldn't have you talking to my boys then, could I?" At this he finally opened his eyes to see Mara standing at the foot of the stairs with a shocked look on her face. "I'm sorry, Ms. Thorne. I can't believe I just said that out loud," he apologized. He then noticed Mara smile at him and nod her head as she walked over and took a seat beside him on the couch.

"Its fine, Mr. Walker. Don't worry about it," Jo answered, trying not to sound offended.

"Really, it's the grief talking. I'm confused and over my head with all this school stuff. It was Olive's thing, you know. She did all of it," he admitted.

"I know, Mr. Walker. Olive and I knew each other quite well, in the school setting, that is. I work with Ben once a week; he is in my buddies group at school. I also work with the kindergarteners. I like to make sure they are all adjusting to school, and I help with any worries they might have. That is why I offered to talk to the boys, because they both know me. Helping kids deal with grief is also part of my job, so ... I'd just really like to help," Jo explained softly.

Simon took a deep breath, he did feel like this woman was trying to help him, and he could use help, especially when it came to his boys. It might do them good to talk to someone besides him or Mara about what they were feeling. "Okay, yes," he agreed, "Thank you for your offer. I think it might be good for them to talk to someone." He looked over at Mara as he said this and saw her smile.

"Great," Jo responded brightly, "I could come by your house tomorrow at 9, or if you'd rather, we could meet at the school?"

Simon didn't want to make the boys go back, not just yet, even if they weren't actually going to be attending classes, so he told her, "The house, the house is fine. You have our address?"

"Yes," Jo said, "I have it right here in front of me. I'll see you tomorrow then, 9 o'clock."

"See you then. Goodbye."

"Goodbye, Mr. Walker."

Simon hung up the phone and looked over at Mara to explain, "School counselor."

"Oh," Mara said, eyebrows raised, "Already, huh? What'd she have to say?"

Simon smiled, sharing, "After avoiding her calls for the past week, I thought I'd better face her. She wants to talk with the boys, see how they are doing. Get an idea of when they'll be ready to go back to school. I'm not sure, do you think it's too early?"

"We can't let them hide out forever, Simon. I think you did a good thing, deciding they should talk to her. It's important to get on with life, even if we don't want to. It's what Olive would want too, you know. She wouldn't want them missing out or falling behind."

"You're right," Simon agreed, looking at Mara. He wondered how she was doing. She had lost her only child, her daughter. They had both been so busy taking care of the boys that he hadn't had a chance to ask her how she was getting along. "How are you doing, Mara?" he asked.

"As good as I can be, I guess," she answered, taking a deep breath, willing herself not to cry, "Olive was my world, especially after her father passed away. It was just her and me for so long. I'm still having a hard time believing she's really gone. I keep thinking she'll just walk through that door." Her voice cracked.

She started to cry, so Simon grabbed the tissues from the coffee table in front of him and set them next to her. "I know what you mean," he said, "I keep waking up at night, wondering where she's gone, and then I remember. Then all I can think is—what am I going to do? What am I going to do without her? She was everything. Everything to this family, to me." He stopped then, knowing if he continued he'd break down again. He didn't have enough energy for that tonight. He was tired of having to pull himself together, to pretend things were okay.

Grabbing more tissues, Mara wiped her nose and said, "She loved you, Simon. Really loved you. I could see it in her. Whenever you or the boys were around, her eyes would light up. She came alive when you were all together. Never forget that, how much she cared for you"—leaning against the back of the couch, Mara closed her eyes—"I remember the first time she told me about you. You had been on a couple of dates, I think. She called and was all mysterious, telling me she had a surprise. Something good to tell me. So, she walked in later that day, with the biggest smile on her face. 'I've met a guy, Mom. Someone special,' she told me, and I knew. I knew you were special because she had never told me about any other guy she'd been dating. There was a glow about her too whenever she talked about you. It filled the room. Right then and there I said a silent prayer because I knew if you two didn't end up together, I'd be cleaning up the pieces for years to come." Mara smiled, then added, "Oh, and you somehow got her to go camping. That was when I knew for sure she'd fallen for you. She would never have set foot in a tent if she wasn't head over heels."

Simon laughed, recalling, "I remember that trip. She kept saying she was really into camping, but I could tell she couldn't wait for the weekend to be over. I would suggest we go for a hike through the woods or canoeing, and she would be all gung-ho but always come up with something else to do. I ended up canceling our second night on the campground and booking us a hotel. I told her I had gotten the campground reservations wrong. You should have seen her face—pure relief!"

Mara shook her head, thinking of the memories. "She sure was something, wasn't she?" she remarked, looking at the pile of tissues in her hand and then sighing. "We'll get through this, Simon. We'll all make it through. We're lucky because we have each other. Thank you for making room for me here, with you and the boys. I don't want to think about what getting through this would be like if I were alone."

"Actually," Simon said, "I want to ask you something, but I don't want you to feel pressured. It's a thought I had a couple of days ago. I'm just going to put it out there. Feel free to shoot me down. Honestly"—he smiled at Mara—"What would you think about staying with us for a while?" Seeing Mara's shocked expression, he continued, "It's just that you've been great with the boys since Olive . . . and they love you, and I just don't think . . . I'm not sure I can do this alone. Not right now anyway. I know it's not your responsibility but—"

Mara raised her hand, cutting him off midsentence, "Stop right there, Simon." She paused for a moment then said, "I would love to."

"Really? Are you sure?" Simon asked quickly, studying Mara's face. "I know it's a lot to ask, and you have your own things to take care of, but . . ." He trailed off as Mara scooted over and gave him a big hug.

"I am absolutely sure, Simon. Thank you for asking." She pulled back and smiled at him sadly, then added, "I spoke to one of my neighbors earlier today. Asked them to look after the house, pick up the mail."

"You did?" Simon asked and then swallowed loudly. "Did you tell them about . . . ?"

Mara nodded, wiping away tears that wouldn't stop flowing. "I gave them your address. They are going to mail anything that looks important here—bills, etc. I hope that's okay."

"Of course. I'm so sorry, Mara," Simon whispered.

Mara shook her head, declaring, "It's not your fault, you know that. I'm not ready to leave you boys yet, anyway. So again, thank you for asking. It's so nice to be around family during difficult times." She paused and took a deep breath. After letting it out, she said, "I think, well, I hope, that we can all help each other start to heal."

"Thank you, Mara. Thank you," Simon said, smiling a real, true smile. "The boys are going to be very excited."

Mara smiled, thinking of her grandsons, then stood up slowly, announcing quietly, "Time for bed." She patted Simon's shoulder and walked down the hall to the guest room.

"Good night, Mara," Simon softly stated.

He knew he should go to bed too. He was tired, and he should try to get some sleep before Beckett woke up, crying for him. But he didn't want to feel it, that pain that tore through him at night. The pain that ripped open his heart and made him cry like a baby, even when he tried to stop it. He could feel it coming; with every beat of his heart it got closer. He felt sick.

He stood up and slowly started walking towards the stairs—up, up, up. Time to get some sleep before the pain got too bad, before that monster named grief destroyed him once again.

He had believed in angels once, before all of this. Before Olive had been taken away from him. He wasn't sure anymore though. Doubt was beginning to darken his spirit.

"If you are out there," he whispered into the night, "now's the time to show your face. Now is your time to save me. Please, just say something." He felt his last bit of hope disappear with his words, as he fell into bed. Burying his face in the pillow that still smelt like Olive, he closed his eyes and waited. He could feel it. It was coming.

* * *

Olive saw Simon sobbing into his pillow, and her heart broke again. How many times could your heart break? She thought she'd been through all she could handle, and now this? How could she get past this? How could she fix it?

"The poet, Rumi, once said, 'You have to keep breaking your heart until it opens.'" Michael was there beside her once again. "Once you accept things, Olive, the hurting will slowly stop."

Watching Simon, she quietly explained, "All I want to do is help my family. If I can help them, then I won't hate myself as much for leaving them."

She sensed Michael's light brighten. Then he spoke, "Hate is a strong word, Olive."

"I'm sorry," Olive replied. Her heart lightened a little as she watched Simon slowly drift to sleep, his eyes now dry. "I just miss them so much. I just want to do something to show them that I love them and that I'm okay." She turned away from Simon and looked at Michael, waiting for a response.

She'd been visiting Simon for a while now. She wasn't sure how long because time was different where she was. Everything was kind of suspended, but not...And you could go visit the past and come back again. It was like the idea of time didn't really exist.

She hadn't gone to see the boys yet. She couldn't. It would be too hard for her to not reach out and touch them, kiss them. She had tried to visit her mom once, but when she got near, she could hear Mara crying quietly, and it had been too much. She wondered when she would be ready to see her, and the boys. She didn't think she would really ever be ready, but not seeing them again was an even worse prospect.

Michael laughed his musical laugh, commenting, "If you wait until you are ready, Olive, we'd be here forever."

Olive took a startled breath and then remarked, "I'm still not used to the whole mind-reading thing."

To give her peace Michael assured her, "You'll get used to it. It's not really mind reading, Olive. It's our way of communicating. Instead of speaking, we can use our thoughts. Though there are some of us who do have the gift to read minds."

Olive was confused. "But you're speaking to me now, with your voice," she stated.

He smiled, it was a beautiful smile, and it made Olive happy.

He explained, "Yes, but I don't need to. Neither do you, Olive."

"I don't?" Olive inquired, skeptical, "So how do you say, or I guess—think—what you want others to hear, but keep private thoughts private?"

Michael shimmered. Olive noticed he did this when he was teaching her things. It was as if he was excited.

"You can use your thought energy to put out there what you want others to hear. But honestly, Olive, there isn't anything we need to keep private from each other. There are no judgments here. We are all a perfect piece of Him, and we know it. Everything here is made up of love and light, so there is nothing to hide."

Olive was still a little unsure, even though what Michael was saying made sense in some kind of intuitive way. "So, you can't read each other's minds and find out everyone's deep, dark secrets?"

Michael laughed again and shimmered, "No, Olive. Even if we could, we wouldn't care because there is nothing to hide or be ashamed of here."

Olive nodded, but then a thought came to her. She asked, "So how can you read my mind? I'm not putting thoughts out there with energy. I have no clue how to do that."

More shimmering, then: "Actually, you are."

"What?" Olive asked, surprised.

"You've always been able to, Olive, but on Earth you lost a little of that ability because you didn't use it there. Now you're back, and even though you don't know it, you *are* putting out some thought energy. It's like listening to a staticky radio station; I get bursts here and there," he explained.

"Back?" she asked, confused again. "What do you mean 'back'?"

Michael was getting excited, he was getting bright. He answered, "Back here, where we are now."

Olive squinted her eyes against the light. "Wait. I was here before?"

Michael dimmed himself a little and stated, "Yes, this is where you came from."

Olive was taken off-guard and almost wanted to deny what he had told her, but there was something inside of her that wanted to shout out, "YES! YES! YES!" She searched her mind for any memory of this place, but there wasn't anything. Not yet. "Wait," she said, "if you are only getting bursts here and there of my thoughts, then how do you always know what I mean?"

Michael smiled, he was having fun. "*I* actually can read minds," he revealed.

"What? But you said ..." Olive trailed off, not sure if she should be offended. She was just plain-old confused.

Michael came closer and touched her shoulder. "It's my gift. I'm special," he explained, "And so are you." He paused, then added, "There is something you can do. To help your family."

Olive snapped to attention. "There is?" she asked, baffled.

"Yes," he said with a smile, "But it only works if they are receptive to it."

Olive nodded, impatiently waiting for more.

"I suggest we try your boys first." When he saw the apprehensive look on Olive's face, he smiled. "Children are much more open to this type of communication. It takes longer with adults. They can be ... difficult." He brightened and then asked, "Are you ready?"

When Olive nodded, he gave her peace, took her hand, and pulled her through.

4

OLIVE BLINKED. THEY WERE IN BEN'S ROOM, AT THE FOOT OF HIS BED.
Olive closed her eyes; it hurt too much to look at him.

"Open your eyes, Olive," instructed Michael. His voice was warm, and it made Olive feel safe.

She opened her eyes and took in the sleeping form of her son. He was lying on his side, knees tucked close to his belly. His brown hair was ruffled, and his eyelashes looked miles long against his rosy cheeks. He was holding his favorite stuffed snake, multi-colored and missing an eye. He had christened it "Cheese Whip" when he had brought it home, though Olive had no idea why.

"He's perfect," Olive whispered.

Michael grew brighter, agreeing, "He is."

Michael smiled down at Ben, and Olive could feel how much Michael loved him. The feeling was so strong, it took her breath away. "Do you really love him that much?" Olive asked, amazed.

"Of course," Michael replied, simply.

"I—I don't understand," she stuttered, "He's not even yours. How can you love him like that?"

"It's who I am. It's who you are too, Olive. It's just that you've forgotten." He smiled, shimmering.

Olive just stared at him. She shook her head, questioning, "What?"

"We are all made up of pure love, from pure love. There is no way that I can't feel love like that because it is who I am. It's my natural way, as is yours." He looked at her confused face, promising, "You'll understand soon."

"I don't know," she responded, thoughts racing. What he was telling her seemed impossible to believe, but there was something there in the back of her mind that she couldn't quite grasp.

"I can show you," Michael said. He was very bright now. Olive could feel him getting brighter. "It might help you remember."

"Okay," Olive agreed. She felt afraid, but she also felt curious.

Michael put his hand on her shoulder, and he gave her peace. "I need you to trust me," he urged, reaching out his hand. "Take my hand. This might hurt a little, but I promise it will be okay. Are you ready?" he asked.

Olive felt his peace. She took his hand and nodded, trusting him.

Michael slowly raised his hand to her chest and placed it on her heart. For a second she felt nothing, but then it came to her, like a bolt of lightning to her chest. She cried out in pain, it felt like her heart was going to explode. She was about to step away when she felt Michael pull back just the tiniest bit, and then it didn't hurt as much.

She could feel it, the way he felt. It hurt, but it wasn't a bad hurt. It was like when she was thinking of her boys, and how her heart would feel so big, like it couldn't contain her love. Like it might burst.

The feeling was so strong, it was hard to take in. It made her cry. It was so bright and big and beautiful, and this was the way he felt about everybody. Every single person. It was amazing. She could see that when he looked at a person, all he saw was their beauty. All he could see was how their heart shined.

After a few moments, he slowly took his hand away and broke the connection, giving Olive time to catch her breath.

"That was beautiful," Olive remarked when she was ready to speak. She felt light, full of energy. It felt good.

Michael laughed, and then he turned his gaze towards Ben, who was still sleeping soundly. "Are you ready to try this?" he asked.

Olive looked at her son. She longed to hold him, to hug him. To see him smile at her. "What exactly are we going to try?" she asked.

"I want you, your spirit, to try to meet his spirit," he shimmered.

Olive felt afraid. She knew nothing about spirits.

Michael laughed kindly, remarking, "Oh, Olive, don't you know? You *are* spirit."

Scared, Olive looked down at herself. She saw her body, her legs, feet, hips, chest—all of it. "If I'm a spirit, then why do I still have my body?" she challenged.

"You still have your body because it's helping you heal. You don't actually need it, and it's not actually there," Michael told her and then gave her peace.

"But I can feel it, I can feel my body," Olive insisted.

"Of course you can," Michael answered. He shimmered. He sent her love.

"If I don't have a body, then how can I feel it?" she asked, afraid. She felt his love and accepted it.

"Because you believe you can," he answered.

"What?" she asked, anxiously.

Michael touched her shoulder, explaining, "Your beliefs make your reality, Olive."

"I still don't understand," she replied, feeling herself calm down.

"That's okay. It'll come to you." He smiled.

"So how do I do this?" she asked, looking at Ben. He started to stir in his sleep, he cried out quietly.

"Is he okay?" Olive asked, alarmed.

"He's fine," Michael assured her. "He can sense us. Like I said before, children are much more open. They still believe that anything is possible."

"Is he going to be afraid, when I . . . ?" Olive wasn't sure how to phrase it. She felt apprehensive now. She didn't want to hurt her son. Michael smiled at her, and she knew instantly that Ben would be okay.

"He might be a little fearful at first, or surprised. Sometimes the feeling of another spirit trying to communicate with you is scary, but it won't hurt him. He will be happy you came," Michael told her, all the while looking at Ben. "Close your eyes, Olive, and see if you can feel his energy. That is how we will start."

Olive drifted a little closer towards Ben and closed her eyes. She inhaled his familiar scent and smiled. Then she felt it, a kind of vibration that reminded her of Ben. She opened her eyes and smiled at Michael. "I feel it," she announced excitedly.

Michael laughed and got brighter. "That's his spirit. When you close your eyes again, I'm going to give you some light. It will help you connect with him. It will feel warm. When you feel it, imagine yourself floating up to meet his energy. You will know his spirit, just like how you know his face. You can connect with him then, but be gentle. If you come on too strong, he could get scared and close himself off from you."

Olive felt herself shaking. "I'm afraid," she admitted.

"Don't be"—Michael smiled, filling her with love—"I'm here."

"What do I do when we meet?" Olive asked, wondering if there was a special trick she needed to remember.

Michael shimmered. It looked as though he was surrounded with swirling pixie dust. "Just talk to him, Olive. Tell him you love him. Tell him you're okay. I'm sure he'll have questions for you. Answer them."

"But I don't know . . ." Olive trailed off, unsure. More peace came.

"It's time," Michael stated, nodding towards Ben, who looked like he might wake up any second. "Close your eyes, and wait for the light. You can do this, Olive."

Deciding she could be brave for her son, she closed her eyes. She felt Ben's energy. It was all around her. She felt warm. Really, really warm. She felt herself floating higher and higher until she saw his face. Ben's face. There he was!

She felt him jump, startled, afraid. She felt his heart speed up, she heard him cry out. Louder this time than before. She reminded herself to be gentle and to let the love she felt for him softly flow from her heart to his. His breathing grew even as he calmed down.

"Mama?" he asked.

"Ben!" she said and smiled, and in his dream she hugged him.

* * *

He was scared, afraid. There was something there, in his room, and it felt weird. He tried to wake up, to see what it was, but he was so tired he couldn't make his eyes open. He was going to try again, but then he felt it. Something was making his heart feel really big and happy. He hadn't felt like that since before his mom had died. It felt nice. He felt something run down his check. He wiped it away and realized he was crying. He missed his mom, he wished she could come back to him. He sniffed quietly and grabbed his stuffed snake, drifting back to sleep.

He was dreaming when he saw her. "Mama?" he asked.

"Ben!" she said, smiling. She hugged him.

It felt so good, he never wanted to let go. "Mom, is it really you?" he asked, his voice muffled, his face pressed into her shoulder.

"Yes," she told him, resting her forehead on his unruly hair, breathing him in.

He let go slowly, stepping back to look at her. "You look different, you're all shiny and stuff. But you look the same too." He smiled.

She smiled back, telling him, "I love you, Ben. I'm so sorry I had to go."

His smiled faded. "Are you okay?" he asked seriously, squinting his eyes. "You're just so bright!"

Olive laughed, explaining, "I'm so bright because I'm so happy to see you." She paused, taking him in, then added, "Yes, I am okay. I miss you very much. I miss your brother and Dad and Gizzy too. Are you okay?"

Ben frowned, he bit his lip, he was trying not to cry. "I'm okay, Mom, but I wish you could come back. You're the only one who understands about school. No one understands now. How will things be okay if I don't have any-one who understands?" He took a big breath and continued, "I'm trying to be strong for Dad and Beckett. I think I'm doing a good job. I haven't cried in front of them..."

Olive's heart hurt when he said this. She responded, "Oh, Ben, I believe you are being strong for them, but you don't need to be. It's okay to cry, even in front of Dad and Beckett and Gizzy. Maybe if you share how you feel or cry, and they see it, well...then it might be easier for them to do the same. Sometimes being strong is being able to show your emotions to others, so they don't feel so alone."

He looked up at her, his eyes wet, and asked, "Really? They won't think I'm a baby?"

"I don't think so, Ben. I think it will actually help them." Olive saw there was still a sliver of doubt in his eyes. "Just try it once, that's all I'm asking." She smiled when she saw his doubt fall away. "I know school is hard, and I know I was the person who was there for you and who understood it all. There are other people, Ben, who can help you."

"Like who?" he asked.

"Dad," she answered, "Gizzy."

"Mom," he asserted impatiently, "I need someone who *gets* me."

"I know someone, but she's not in our family. So you'll have to do your best to trust me on this," Olive said encouragingly.

"Who?" Ben asked, surprised.

"Ms. Thorne," Olive told him, "I know she's a teacher, and maybe it's not cool to be friends with a teacher, but...I can tell she really cares about you, Ben. She really wants to help."

Ben was quiet for a while, thinking about what his mom had said. "Okay," he agreed finally, "She is nice, and she is pretty like you. But how do I . . . how do I ask her?"

Olive studied Ben. His big, serious eyes. His messy hair. He was getting so big, so old. He had a yearning to do what was right and always be his best, and she was so proud of him. He worked so hard in school, only to fall behind what was considered 'normal' for his grade level. He was smart though. Wonderfully and amazingly smart. Only he didn't always feel like he was.

It made her angry that when a child learned in a different way, the school wasn't expected to change the way they taught; the child was expected to change the way they learned. This wasn't fair, and it broke her heart. She experienced firsthand how a child's confidence suffered because of this. Wasn't a school's job to teach kids, not to make them feel bad about themselves?

There'd been many a time that Olive wanted to march into that school and pronounce, "You aren't doing your job! He is suffering and there has to be something you can do! You are failing him!" She knew that getting worked up would help with nothing though.

So she had done all that a parent could do. She'd gotten him professionally evaluated. Then, finally the ball had started to roll, and Ben had been given extra help in math, writing, and reading. Olive had been surprised that it had been so difficult to get her child help in school. Her thoughts had been that if a child needed help, they should get help, as simple as that. She had also been surprised at all they had had to do, from full school evaluations, to a doctor's diagnosis, to even more expensive evaluations. Thank goodness they'd had the money to do it. She'd had no idea what a parent would do if they couldn't afford it.

When Ben had been diagnosed with dyslexia, Olive had been startled to learn that not many teachers at his school knew much about it. They'd known ways to help with anxiety or anger or attention and had a long list of accommodations that went along with those needs, but when faced with questions on how to help him with his dyslexia, they'd never really had an answer. Their lack of knowledge about dyslexia had floored Olive, but things had been going well at school this year, so she had kept her focus on the positive.

Olive smiled at Ben. He was perfect in her eyes. She suggested, "When you go back to school, you could talk to Ms. Thorne after your buddies group. Tell her you'd like her help. She'll understand, she knows how things are, Ben."

He smiled, admitting, "I think I can do that."

"I think so too," Olive agreed. She could hear Michael now. He was calling her, telling her it was time to go.

Surprisingly, Ben heard it too. "What was that?" he asked.

"That's my friend, Michael. He's been helping me here. He's the one who brought me to you," she explained quietly, taking Ben in. She didn't want to leave him yet.

"So you're okay where you are? You aren't hurt?" Ben asked again.

"I'm okay, Ben. Sometimes my heart hurts when I miss you guys, but Michael is helping me. He is who I go to when I'm afraid or don't know what to do."

"I don't want you to be sad, Mom. I love you," Ben said, smiling sadly at Olive.

"I have an idea," Olive announced brightly. "I'll do my best here to be happy if you do your best too. Remember, it's okay to cry and talk about how we feel. I've been doing that where I am, and it feels good. It helps me feel better."

Ben nodded in agreement. Then he asked, "Mom, will you please try to come back?" His eyes were big and full of hope.

"I'll do my best, Ben. I love you so much." Olive hugged him once more, relishing the feeling of his body in her arms.

"Bye, Mom. I love you," Ben said.

"Bye Ben!," she called out, and then she was gone.

Ben was sad when she left, but he felt happy too. He was able to talk to his mom! He fell back into a deeper sleep, dreaming of angels. An especially bright and sparkly one kept whispering jokes to Ben, making him laugh.

* * *

He was dreaming when he saw his mommy. She walked right onto the pirate ship he was commandeering, and she gave him some ice cream.

"Mommy!" Beckett cried, hugging her tight.

"Hello, my sweetie," Olive said, hugging him back. She wished she could hold on forever.

"Mommy! What are you doing here? I'm fighting the bad pirates, see?" He pointed excitedly towards a pirate-filled ocean. Boats were bobbing along with the waves.

"I see," Olive replied. "Would you take a break for some ice cream?"

"Yes!" Beckett shouted, and all at once the boats disappeared, and they were at his favorite park, sitting on a bench.

"Wow," Olive noted, "You are a good dreamer!"

Beckett smiled, then licked his ice cream cone, and asked, "Mom, how'd you get here?"

Olive laughed and answered, "My friend Michael brought me. He's the one who helps me when I need help."

Beckett licked his cone. Then he inquired, "Is he that sparkly angel guy over there?"

Olive was surprised at what her boys could see. "Yes, that's him," she confirmed.

Beckett laughed. "He's funny," he commented.

Olive's heart felt big. She loved Michael for making her boys happy. "I like to see you laugh," she told him, ruffling Beckett's blond hair.

Beckett set his cone down. "Mommy," he began, "I miss you, and I am so sad that you're gone. I wish you could come home."

Olive took his hand in hers. "I miss you too, Beckett. I wish I could come home, but I can't. I love you so much, and I'm sorry that I had to go."

"Why can't you come back, Mommy? Ask that bright funny guy to take you home." He looked like he was about to cry.

She smiled, wanting to make him happy. "I did ask, but he said no. Do you know who else I asked?" she continued, hoping to make him smile again.

He shook his head, his hair flying in all directions. "Who?"

Olive bent down and whispered in his ear.

Beckett's eyes got huge. "Really?" he asked, his smile back, "What was He like?"

"Bright, brighter than him," she explained, pointing towards Michael, "and He could take away my hurts too. Like when I was feeling really, really sad, He took it away, so I could feel a little better."

"Really," Beckett remarked, eyes bigger than before. He picked up his cone, asking, "So you feel better now?"

Olive shrugged and replied, "I still miss you guys a lot, but I am better than I was."

Beckett looked thoughtful. Then he inquired, "Do you think it's okay if I go away from Daddy now?"

"What do you mean?" Olive asked.

"At first I didn't want him to leave me because I was scared. So I didn't let Dad do anything without me. But now that you've come to see me, I'm not scared anymore. I know you're okay"—he looked at Michael, then laughed— "He said it's okay to be happy, even if you aren't here. Is that okay, Mommy? Is it okay if I laugh, even if you're gone? Can I leave Dad and do things by myself now?"

Beckett set his cone down again, and Olive took his face in her hands. She told him, "I love you, Beckett. I want so much for you to be happy. So please laugh, as much as you can! If I know you are laughing, it will make me happy too."

"It will?" he asked, wiggling out of her hands.

Olive nodded, adding, "It's good to have time alone and time with family. You don't have to be afraid anymore, so you can be how you were when I was there, okay? Because I am okay, and even though you can't see me, I'm still here."

Olive watched Beckett. He nodded. She could see the fear leave him, and she noticed how much lighter he felt without it. She heard Michael calling.

Beckett, hearing it too, requested, "Mommy, please come back to visit."

She pulled him in for a big hug, responding, "I'll try to come back. I love you Beckett."

"I love you, Mommy," he stated and then tilted his head up and gave her a kiss on the cheek.

Then she was gone.

Beckett missed his mommy, but he was happy that she was okay. He wasn't afraid that someone was going to take his dad away anymore because the angel had promised that his dad would be safe. Beckett liked the angel. He'd told Beckett to call for him if he wanted to talk again. Then he had given Beckett some of his sparkly stuff. He had put it under Beckett's pillow and said it could help him fight the bad pirates. It made him feel warm and happy, it felt like love. Beckett drifted into a deeper sleep, dreaming of angels, the sparkly one making him laugh.

5

THE FIRST THING SIMON REALIZED WHEN HE WOKE UP WAS THAT HE was alone. Beckett wasn't snuggled up beside him. There were no knees pressing into his back or arms slung around his neck. This was the first night in weeks that he had slept entirely through.

Hoping everything was okay, he crept quietly into Beckett's room, then Ben's. Simon breathed a sigh of relief, reassured that both boys were still breathing and safe. Walking down the hall, he caught a whiff of Mara's rich coffee and smiled. If he was lucky, he could make it downstairs and grab a cup before it was gone. He didn't want to press his luck, but today seemed to be off to a good start. He hoped it would stay that way.

Walking downstairs and into the kitchen, Simon smiled at Mara as she set two cups of coffee onto the table beside a heaping plate of buttered toast. "Mara, you're an angel," he announced, sitting down and taking a long sip. "Aahh, still the best coffee around."

Mara laughed. "You're chipper this morning," she observed, opening the fridge and pulling out some creamer.

"I am," he replied, leaning back against his chair, "I have good reason to be too. Beckett slept all night long in his own bed."

Mara smiled as she stirred in her creamer, then set her spoon down on the napkin beside her coffee mug. "Cheers to small victories," she pronounced, raising her steaming mug towards Simon.

"Cheers," he repeated happily as they clinked their mugs together. He grabbed a piece of toast. "How was your night?" he asked between bites.

Mara smiled softly as she wrapped her hands around her mug, warming them. She answered, "You know, it was okay." She paused, then added, "This might sound odd, but I had the strongest feeling of Olive last night. It was like she was here, in the house. I woke up with a kind of knowing that she is okay. That she is healing"—she studied Simon—"I hope I didn't put a damper on your morning. It's just that when I think of her now, I don't feel as sad. I still

39

miss her, of course, but I just feel deep within that she is okay, and she wants us to be okay."

Simon took a big gulp of coffee, it burnt his throat. He felt himself tear up just thinking of Olive. He missed her so much. Sometimes it was a struggle just to breathe. What Mara had told him brought back his memory of calling out for some kind of sign last night. He had meant for the sign to be for him, not Mara. He was the one who had called out for proof, so why hadn't he gotten any?

"Simon," Mara said, kindly. She could tell he was struggling and regretted bringing up Olive at that moment. He had been having a good morning, and she felt like she had ruined it. "I'm sorry, Simon. I can see you're hurting. I only brought it up because I was hoping it might make you feel better to know she is okay."

Simon could see Mara's regret. He could tell she wanted to help him. He cleared his throat and replied, "Don't be sorry, Mara, please." He paused, not wanting to cry. "How do you know?" he asked. "How do you *really* know that she is okay? I just don't understand it. How can you feel her, but I can't?"

"I don't have all the answers, Simon," Mara replied. "I have no idea how I know, I just do. When I think about Olive, instead of feeling grief, I feel peace. I feel happy. That's the only way I can describe it"—she looked at him and could tell he was hurting—"I know one day you'll feel it too, Simon. It'll take time, but you will." She leaned forward and took his hand in hers, promising, "I'm here for you, Simon, whatever you need. I want to help, not just the kids, but you too."

He took Mara's hand and squeezed it gently, saying, "Thank you, Mara. I don't know what I would do if you weren't here"—he blinked away a couple of tears—"It's still so unreal that she's gone. I keep waiting for her to walk down the stairs or call me up to talk about the boys, but she doesn't. That will never happen again, and it's so hard to face. I don't know how I'm going to do it alone."

Mara smiled, reminding him, "You're not alone, silly. You have me." She stood up and walked to the coffee pot, gently grabbing it off the holder. "More coffee?" she asked.

"Please," he said, as she filled up his mug again, then, "Thank you, Mara, for everything." He took a careful sip and looked up towards the ceiling; someone was jumping on their bed.

"And they're up," Mara remarked with a smile. "We got a few minutes of peace, yes?" She held up her mug once more.

"To small victories," Simon stated with a smile, and they clinked mugs again.

Taking the last sip of her coffee, Mara got up and walked to the stove, where she pulled a big pot off the low-burning back burner. "Boys!" she called, "Breakfast!" She smiled when she heard little feet thundering down the stairs.

Simon looked at the pot questioningly, then inquired, "What's in there?"

Mara laughed, "You're looking at me like I've got three heads. Don't tell me Olive never made you real oatmeal on the stove?"

Simon laughed, uttering, "Olive, cook? The only oatmeal we've ever had was from those little microwave packets." He smiled as Mara jokingly scolded her daughter. He felt a little better, a little bit lighter as he watched the boys come down the stairs and gobble up Mara's oatmeal. *It's nice*, he thought, *to smile and feel good again.* Seeing the boys laughing with their grandma, he thought about Olive. He knew she would have loved this, this little moment of joy. He decided that since she wasn't here to enjoy it, he would enjoy it for her. And with that one thought, his heart began to heal.

* * *

"Guess what, Dad?" Ben asked, dropping his spoon into his empty oatmeal bowl.

"What?" Simon asked, giving Ben a smile. He was thoroughly enjoying this time with the boys.

"I saw Mom last night. She came to visit me." Ben looked at his dad with a huge smile.

Before Simon had a chance to react, Beckett chimed in, "Me too!" He laughed, adding, "That was so cool!"

Simon almost choked on his coffee. He looked over at Mara to see if she had heard the same thing. Maybe he was just hearing things.

"Really?" Mara answered, sensing Simon's shock. "Tell us more." She glanced over at Simon with a look of surprise on her face.

Ben was quiet for a moment, studying his dad's face, trying to read his thoughts.

Beckett wasted no time. He jumped in and told his story, "Well, I was dreaming about fighting the bad guys, and then, all of a sudden, there was Mom! She gave me ice cream, and we talked, and there was an angel with her that was so funny! He gave me some of his sparkles too!" Beckett's face split into a huge smile, and he laughed, remembering the angel.

"I saw him too," Ben told Beckett, "He was so bright and shiny and funny! I was scared at first because I knew someone was there and I didn't know who. The angel said I didn't need to be afraid, and then I saw Mom. It was really awesome." Ben smiled, his dimples showing.

Simon and Mara exchanged looks. "What did you talk to Mom about, Ben?" Simon asked, his interest piqued.

Ben's eyes lit up as he answered, "We talked about the angel. He helps her a lot. He was the one to bring her to see us. She said she misses us, but she is okay. She wants us to be happy. She told me it's okay to feel sad and cry sometimes when I miss her." He looked at Simon when he said this, and it pulled at Simon's heart.

"Yeah," Beckett broke in, not wanting to be left out. "She told me I don't have to be afraid anymore either. She said it's okay if we're not always together all the time, Dad." Beckett smiled up into Simon's eyes. "I told the angel I was scared that you'd leave too, but he said you won't, Dad."

"Are you okay, Dad?" Ben asked worriedly when he saw Simon beginning to cry.

Simon nodded his head and smiled at his boys. They reminded him so much of Olive it hurt. He was crying because he had gotten his sign. If it hadn't been clear from talking with Mara this morning, it was abundantly clear now. Olive was okay, and she was doing whatever she could to make sure her family was too. That was so like her.

Simon was surprised at how easily he believed his boys. How much he felt that what they were saying was true. He felt it, deep down in his bones. It sounded crazy, what they were saying. If he were to have heard something like this before, he would have chalked it up to an over-active imagination or wishful thinking. But no, he was absolutely sure that his boys had talked to their mom last night. His only question was—why hadn't she come to him?

"Dad?" Ben asked again, snapping Simon out of his thoughts.

Simon got up and gave each of his boys a long, tight hug. "Boys," he said, smiling at them, "I'm okay, but I still miss Mom. Sometimes I miss her so much that I just don't know what I'm going to do. But hearing you tell me about what happened last night makes me so happy. If Mom's watching out for us, then I know we will be okay."

Mara stood up from the table and started to collect the bowls and spoons. "Your mom didn't come to visit me last night, boys, but I did have a feeling she was here," Mara shared as she moved to the sink to rinse out each bowl and place it in the dishwasher. She followed with the spoons. She was surprised to see the boys still sitting at the table, still as ever, waiting to see what else she had to say. "When I woke up this morning, the feeling of your mom was so strong I could almost touch it. I was filled with peace at the thought of her, and I just knew that it was her letting me know that she's okay." Mara smiled at their wide eyes, at their perfect faces.

She saw her daughter in them, all the time. In the way Beckett couldn't hold back when he was excited and in his smile. In Ben's dimples and the shape of his eyes. In the way Ben cared so much for everybody and everything, almost to a point where he hurt from it more than he should. The way Beckett loved, in a fierce, unstoppable way, so fearless. They were so beautiful, they were little pieces of her daughter, and she treasured each moment with them.

Looking at her grandsons brought her back to a memory she had of Olive. Olive had been about five, and she was helping Mara make Rice Krispies treats. While Mara spread out the finished treats into a cake pan, Olive was sitting on the counter, licking the leftover cereal from a giant spoon and scraping that huge spoon into the bowl they used to mix the cereal, butter, and marshmallows together, making sure to get each clump before her mom put the bowl into the sink.

It was in that moment that Mara thought, *This is it. This is what I live for. These normal, everyday, ordinary moments together. Just us talking about nothing, just talking. Being together. This is life.* She realized how easy it was to miss those moments, waiting only for the big things or exciting times to come. She realized that life was full of those little moments. They happen all the time, right in front of your face, and if you're lucky enough to see them, what a beautiful life you can have.

Mara never knew what had caused that flash of realization, but she was grateful for it. It had changed the way she looked at her life. It had made her appreciate everything. She hoped Olive had had some of those moments with her boys. She hoped they hadn't been so darn busy that they'd missed what was right in front of them.

Simon's exclamation pulled her out of her thoughts. "Oh no!" he cried, looking at his watch, "I just remembered, someone from your school is coming over this morning to talk with us." He ran over to the front door and peered out of the window, cursing under his breath. "Hurry, boys! Run upstairs and get dressed. She's here now!" He ran back towards the stairs, feet slippery in his thick socks, sliding out from under him. He managed to catch himself by grabbing onto the stair railing. "Answer the door, will you?" he called to Mara, as he rushed up the stairs, "Tell her we'll be right down!"

Laughing a little at the chaos, Mara wondered if she had enough time to make a mad dash to the guest room to grab a sweater. Her appearance wasn't any better. Seeing someone coming up the sidewalk, she gave up on the sweater, hoping she didn't look too haggard.

"Who is it?" the boys yelled, as they followed their dad up the stairs. "Who's coming over?"

"I can't quite remember!" Simon called, pulling out dresser drawers and throwing clothes onto the floor. "Some lady. I think her name is Miss Claw."

"Miss Claw? Daddy, she sounds scary!" Beckett remarked, sounding a little worried. He pulled on a pair of shorts he found under his bed and a long-sleeved shirt with Yoda on it.

"Dad, there is no Miss Claw!" Ben called out, finding sweats in the corner of his closet and a pajama top behind his desk.

"No, no, that's not it," Simon muttered, grabbing yesterday's t-shirt and giving it a sniff. He winced. "Oh, now I remember, it's Ms. Thorne. She's nice, right?"

Hearing the doorbell, Mara glanced up the stairs, hoping everyone was dressed. She spotted Ben and could have sworn she saw a smile flash across his face when his dad finally remembered who was coming to chat.

* * *

Stepping inside and taking in the haphazard bunch who greeted her in the hall, Jo glanced quickly at her watch to make sure she hadn't gotten the time wrong. "We did agree on 9:00, right?" she asked, smiling at the boys, who seemed surprised to see a teacher in their home.

"Yes, yes, of course," Simon confirmed nervously, gesturing for her to come in. "We just weren't paying much attention to the time this morning …" he trailed off, then added, "It's becoming a bit of a habit around here." He smiled sheepishly at Jo.

Slipping off her shoes, Jo smiled reassuringly back at Simon and then extended her hand towards Mara, who had her hands on the boys' shoulders. She stated, "Hello, I'm Jo Thorne. I work at the school."

Mara stepped forward and took Jo's hand. "Nice to meet you, I'm Mara, Olive's mom and lucky grandma to these two," she said, smiling at Jo, quietly taking stock.

"Well, it's great to meet you," Jo replied warmly. She looked at Ben and Beckett and told them, "Hi, boys, I've missed seeing you at school."

Beckett looked up at her shyly as Ben asked, "Is that why you're here because we've missed school?"

"Are we in trouble?" Beckett asked, sounding excited.

Jo laughed, answering, "No, Beckett, you're not in trouble." She looked at Ben when she explained, "I'm here because I wanted to see how you're doing. I know you're going through a tough time right now, and I wanted to chat with you about it."

"Ohhhh," the boys said in unison.

Everyone was quiet for a beat, then Mara said, "Come in, Jo. We can chat in the family room." She took Beckett's hand and led the way, Ben walking beside Jo and Simon following, looking worried.

Mara took a seat on the couch, with Beckett and Ben sitting on either side of her and Simon sitting beside Ben.

Jo sank into the loveseat across from them and smiled. "Well," she began, letting out a big breath of air, releasing the tension she had been holding onto, "First, let me just say how sorry I am. I very much admired Olive. I wish I'd been able to get to know her more. Whenever I saw her at school, I would make a point to say hello. She was someone I really enjoyed talking with because she was always filled with such positivity"—Jo paused and looked at Ben and Beckett—"One thing I know, is how much she loved you two. She would do anything for you two boys. You know that, right?"

Ben and Beckett nodded, unsure where the conversation was going.

Simon rubbed Ben's back and remarked, "Thank you, Jo. We sure do miss her." He swallowed and willed himself to keep it together.

Jo smiled again, leaning forward slightly to look at Ben and Beckett, and continued, "I want you both to know that when you decide that you are ready to come back to school, I'll be there to help you. If you need a break or just someone to talk to, you can always come to me. It's hard losing someone you love, and it can be hard to move on and get back to your regular life. I want to do whatever I can to make this not so hard"—she looked at the two handsome boys, their faces still unsure—"I won't care if you come into my office because you feel like you might cry and don't want anyone to see you, or if you come because you want to check out what kind of candy I have on my desk. I won't care, and I won't tell anyone either, except maybe your dad."

She caught Ben's eye and smiled, hoping what she had said would make him feel comfortable and motivated to come back to school. She wanted him to trust her, and she wanted him to know there was a safe place for him if things got to be too much.

"What kind of candy?" Beckett asked, interrupting her thoughts.

"You'll just have to come and see," she teased, winking at him.

Simon looked at his boys. Beckett sat wondering what treats were waiting for him back at school. Simon knew he'd be okay going back, but that he was waiting for Ben. It was amazing to Simon that this little guy had an innate knowing of what his brother needed and was willing to do whatever it took to help him.

Beckett was holding them together, but everything hinged on Ben, Simon realized. Maybe they were all moving on and slowly starting to heal in their own ways, but no one would be 100 percent okay until Ben was.

Looking at Ben, Simon could see the hope in his eyes and the longing that everything would be okay. Simon knew how hard school was for Ben, without having to deal with losing the person who'd fought for him the hardest.

He could fight for Ben, push for all the extra help he needed, but he didn't know the ins and outs like Olive had, and he felt grossly inadequate. He knew he needed to get over it and just do what he had to do, but he was overwhelmed and didn't know where to start. That's why he was thankful Jo was here, wanting to help. She obviously knew her stuff and would be exactly what Ben needed right now, until Simon could find his way.

A glimmer of hope ignited inside of Simon's chest as he watched Jo quietly talking to Ben. *This could work*, he thought, *This could really work*. But Ben needed to trust Jo, and the only way that would happen was if she could find a way to spark his belief, like Olive had. They'd just have to wait and see.

A movement in the kitchen caught his eye, and he turned toward it, wondering what it was. Seeing nothing, he shook his head gently, thinking he needed to get his eyes checked. Sensing the movement again, he slowly turned his head, wondering if he was going crazy.

When his eyes found the spot where he had seen something, or thought he'd seen something, his body filled up with a kind of warmth he'd never felt before, and an image of Olive flashed in his mind. "I love you," she said to him, and she took his hands in hers, warming them. Then she was gone.

Dumbfounded, Simon blinked and looked down at his hands, which felt like they were on fire. He jumped when he felt someone's hand on his shoulder.

"Are you okay?" Mara asked quietly. Jo was still talking to the boys in muted tones. They had moved to the floor and were playing checkers, and Mara didn't want to interrupt them.

"This is going to sound crazy," Simon whispered, "But I think I just saw Olive." He nodded towards the kitchen. "Did that really just happen?"

Mara smiled at Simon, about to ask him to tell her about it, when Beckett approached them both.

He looked at Simon and laughed, commenting, "You saw her, didn't you, Daddy? You just saw Mommy over there." He was pointing towards the kitchen. He gave Simon a big hug, then walked back to where Ben and Jo were huddled, joining in their conversation.

Simon and Mara looked at each other in surprise.

Throwing his hands up in the air, Simon admitted, "I have no words for this." He smiled, feeling happier than he had in weeks.

Mara laughed, enjoying the glow on Simon's face, enjoying the connection being built between her grandchildren and this special teacher. "Sometimes the most special things can only be felt by our hearts," she remarked, knowing that this moment, right now, was most definitely something special.

* * *

"I did it!" Olive exclaimed, "I think he felt me!" She smiled at Michael who was shimmering brightly.

Michael smiled back. "It's time," he told her, taking her hand.

Olive shook her head, insisting, "But I want to stay with them. I want to make sure they're okay."

"They are okay, Olive. Just look at them." Michael pointed towards her family. They were all gathered on the floor, laughing at something that Ben had said. Not to be outdone, Beckett told his own joke, which caused a big round of belly laughs, Jo included.

Olive watched her family. She studied her boys, sensing little seeds of trust starting to sprout and grow towards Jo. Olive's heart hurt for just a moment, wishing she could be the one making them smile. The feeling was gone in an instant though, replaced by gratitude for this woman who she hoped could pull the boys out of their pain, help them feel safe and loved.

"I'm happy she's there," Olive stated quietly. "I'm surprised it doesn't hurt as much . . . another woman sitting where I usually would." She looked at Michael. He smiled at her, letting her figure it out for herself, letting her feel it. "I just want them to be happy, and I think she can help," Olive added, looking at them again, feeling her heart fill with love. She missed them so much. What she wouldn't give to hug them, really hug them. She'd never let go. It was hard, this feeling of homesickness, longing for something she knew she'd never have again. It was almost too much, almost. But this time, instead of looking to Michael for help, she felt her way through it, forcing herself to believe that someday, someway, things would get easier.

She felt Michael take her hand and pull her through, and then she was back where she came from once again.

6

"Olive," He said gently.

She was still getting used to Him, getting used to how He could make her feel so bright and full of love. She always knew when He was near because the love she felt coming from Him was so amazing it almost hurt. He was so much, He was joy and peace and kindness and compassion and love and acceptance and creativity and an infinite number of things. She sometimes cried when He was around because it was all too much to take in. She didn't cry because she was sad though; she was cried because it was all so beautiful.

"Olive," He said again, and she closed her eyes, so she could feel Him. "You've been doing well, Olive. I'm so proud of you. You have made sure your family is okay, and you were able to connect with them. Not everyone can do that as easily as you have. Your love for your family is so inspiring."

"Thank you," she replied.

"You've done all that you've needed to do, Olive. It's time to move on now," He explained, surrounding her with warmth and light.

Olive was surprised, asserting, "What do you mean, 'move on'? I can still visit them, right? I told my boys I'd be back!"

"It's time to move on, Olive. It's time to do what you've come here to do. We need you, Olive." He took the piece of the plan that was meant for her and laid it out for her to see.

She wasn't ready to leave her family, and she didn't want to see the plan. She looked at it anyway but found she couldn't read what it said. "Please," she begged, "just give me some more time. Just a little more time with them." She felt herself crying.

He looked at her. He knew she wasn't quite ready. He loved her and wanted her to be happy. "You have a little more time, Olive, but remember, if you want them to move on, you need to move on too."

He smiled at her, and she felt His love pouring down around her. She saw herself reflected in His eyes and saw how much He wanted her to be happy and how perfect she was to Him. In that moment she felt completely loved and pure, and she knew that she was meant to do great things. She knew He had given her a gift when He had given her more time with her family. She believed Beckett would be okay, she believed her mom would be okay, she even thought Simon would be okay. She wanted to use her time to make sure Ben had what he needed, before she was pulled away completely.

He was gone, and Michael was beside her, smiling, shimmering, and golden.

"I want to make sure Ben is okay before I move on," she told him. "How much time do I have?"

"Only as much as you need," Michael answered, pulling her through again.

* * *

They were in Ben's classroom at school, and as the surroundings came into view, Michael gave her peace.

She wondered why he had chosen this moment to fill her with peace, but then she noticed that Ben was sitting at his desk, head down. He was crying.

"What happened?" she asked Michael, feeling his sorrow as Ben's tears continued to fall.

Michael shook his head. Olive was surprised to see that he looked sad. Because Michael had never looked less than beautifully happy, she wondered what was causing his pain.

"There is so much love all around, but not everyone can see it. There are also so many people suffering, and sometimes these people think the only way to feel better is to hurt someone else. But this only causes more pain for everyone involved. My wish is that everyone could see how much beauty they have within. I believe if that happened, all the hurting and sadness would come to an end"—Michael sighed—"This is a lesson we all have to learn when we are on Earth, to love each other. We are all connected by love. If we hurt someone else, it's like we are hurting ourselves."

Olive understood what Michael was saying, but she wasn't sure what it had to do with Ben until she heard it.

Raising her head, she looked over to where Ben was sitting, and she saw the boy whose desk was behind Ben's. She saw the boy lean forward and whisper in Ben's ear, "Hey baby, what are you crying about, you wimp? You crying because your mama is dead? Dumb baby."

She saw the boy next to Ben join in, "No, he's just crying because he's too stupid to know how to read. He's probably too stupid to know his mom's gone too. He's dumb, he goes to that special class for dumbos."

The first boy laughed. "Hey, Dumbo!" he delivered and hit Ben on the top of the head. "Do you like your new name, Dumbo?"

Olive looked at Ben, distraught, wondering what had caused these boys to lash out. Who would be so cruel? She waited for Ben to say something, for him to stand up for himself or at least go talk to the teacher. But no, he just sat there, head down, shoulders shaking, tears flowing, trying to disappear.

Olive wished she could hug him. She would give absolutely anything if she could come back to life for five minutes, just to hug him. She wanted him to know that she was there and that she loved him more than anything. She wanted to make him feel better. She wanted to take his face in her hands and wipe his tears away. She wanted to wrap her arms around him and simply hold him, but she couldn't because she was dead. She was gone, and the *only* thing she wanted to do wasn't possible. She thought of all the times she hadn't hugged him when she could have, and she felt sick. She thought of all the moms that were alive and able to hug their kids today. She felt sicker. She thought of all the moms who could have hugged their kids today and didn't. She felt furious.

Olive had never been this mad in her life. She didn't know she could be this mad when she was a spirit or ghost or whatever she was. She felt like she was on fire. She wanted to take those mean boys by their necks and slam their heads together until they decided to be nice.

She felt Michael beside her, felt him give her peace, give her love, but she didn't want it right now. She swung her head around to see what the teacher was doing. The teacher was correcting papers while everyone else was supposed to be reading, but obviously not *everybody* was following instructions.

Olive felt herself beginning to fly into a rage. She flew over to where the teacher was sitting quietly at her desk and screamed as loud as she could in the teacher's face. Nothing happened. Olive felt like an angry ghost, whooshing around trying to wreak havoc. She laughed a little when she realized that's exactly what she was.

She heard Michael call her, but she ignored him, her anger still pumping in her nonexistent veins. She took a big breath and screeched at the teacher again. This time the teacher blinked and raised her eyes, looking around the classroom to see who had made a noise. Not noticing anything, not even glancing in Ben's direction, she went back to her papers.

This made Olive even more furious. So Olive took her hand and swept it over the desk, surprising herself when the neatly stacked tests flew off the desk in a huff.

Surprised, the teacher jumped up, causing her chair to smash into the wall behind her. At that exact moment she saw one of the boys swat Ben on the back of the head with his pencil. She noticed Ben with his head down, and she wondered if this had been going on for a while. Judging from his red face and shaking shoulders, it had been. "Vance!" the teacher shouted, "Get over here. You too, Boston." Her face was red, and she gave 'the eye' to any student who dared look at her. She should have been paying better attention. She knew Ben was going through a hard time.

Olive was glad the boys had been caught, but she wasn't done with them yet. When the boys stood up by the teacher's desk, listening to their punishment, Olive was busy tying their shoelaces together. When they turned around to start their walk to the principal's office, their legs got tangled up together and they both came crashing down to the floor, a head and a nose colliding.

The other students attempted to stifle their laughter as the boys tried to untangle themselves from each other. One rubbing his head, the other holding his nose, trying to stop the blood from flowing out.

The teacher sighed, pulling both boys up and marching them out the door. "I'll be right back, class. Please keep it down and continue reading!" she called out, grabbing some tissues and handing them to the nose bleeder.

Olive looked at Ben. His face was still red, his eyes were still wet, but he had a small smile on his face. Almost like he knew what had happened. If Olive couldn't hug her son, she could at least protect him. She decided to stick around school and do exactly that.

Turning to Michael to tell him her plan, she saw for the first time another emotion she didn't think he would ever show. Anger. Studying him a little longer, she realized it wasn't anger she saw in him, but deep sadness and disappointment. In her.

"Michael," she began, "I'm sorry. I just wanted to help my son."

"Olive," Michael responded, his shimmer not so shimmery, "that's not who we are. That's not who *you* are. I know you want to help Ben, but that's not the way."

He looked at her sadly, then put his hand on her shoulder. She felt his forgiveness. She also felt his sorrow for Ben and for the two boys that were being mean. To him, they weren't mean boys, they were boys that were hurting. They were boys that desperately needed love because they so rarely got it at home. He felt their pain, and it became his pain, as did Ben's pain and Olive's.

"Hate doesn't cure hate, Olive. Only love does that." He brightened a little as he looked at Ben, he blessed him, then continued, "Ben's struggle might seem hard to bear, Olive, but I promise you he is strong enough to overcome anything that gets thrown at him. He was given this life because he is strong enough to live it."

Olive started to cry. She knew it was true, but she still didn't want him going through things that might hurt him. She loved him so much.

"Ben is a beautiful child, Olive. He is so special and he is going to do so many amazing things in his life. But the only way for him to do those amazing things is for him to go through some hard times and then learn and grow from them"—he gave her peace, filling her with love and light—"It will be hard for you, but you need to let him suffer those growing pains. You need to let him grow into all that he is going to be. The key is that *you* need to *let him* do it."

"I feel like I messed everything up," Olive admitted. "I only listened to my anger and didn't care about anything else. I don't want to leave him now. I don't want the last time I see him to be when I was angry. I want it to be filled with peace."

Michael smiled. He was getting shimmery again. "I think you are beginning to understand. You still have time, Olive. Use it wisely."

* * *

As Ben walked out of the principal's office and down the hall towards his locker, he thought about what had happened in class earlier. He hated Boston and Vance for being so mean to him. He didn't understand what their problem was. He was always nice to them, always went along with their games, even if he thought they were a little dumb. He just wanted to get along.

Then this had happened. The only thing that kept it from ranking as one of the top five worst days of his life was that he was almost 100 percent sure his mom had been there. He hadn't seen her, but he *had* felt her. And he was pretty sure she was the one who had tied Boston and Vance's shoelaces together. He had no clue *how* she had done it; he just knew she had.

Thinking of her made him smile. He kind of liked having a ghost on his side. If he could choose, he would for sure choose his mom in real life, but … now she was kind of like a super hero. All invisible and stealth and butt-kicking.

As he rounded the corner, he saw his dad and Beckett talking to Ms. Thorne. He heard Beckett laugh, and he felt happy. He wasn't sure how he was going to make it through the year with kids in school being mean and his mom being gone, and him having a hard time with math and reading. But he was sure of one thing though, and that was that they were all going to be okay. They had each other, and right now, that was all that mattered.

"Hey, bud!" his dad called out as Ben approached. He was holding Ben's backpack, and when Ben got close enough, he tossed it to him. "Think fast," he teased.

Ben laughed as he just barely caught his bag. He liked seeing his dad happy.

"What do you think about going out for pizza? We can go to Saucy Baby," Simon asked Ben and Beckett. Saucy Baby was their favorite pizza place. He liked it because the food was amazing, and the boys liked it because of the arcade.

Ben's day had been, well, not the best he'd ever had, and Simon wanted to cheer him up. They had talked about what had happened with the principal, gotten everything worked out. Simon just wanted to move on, and he was pretty sure Ben did too. He hoped this would help.

"Yeah!" Beckett cried, "But only if we can do the arcade." He looked up at Simon pleadingly.

Ben smiled, agreeing, "Yeah, can we please go to the arcade, Dad?" He put his bag over his shoulder, waiting for an answer.

Jo turned to Simon and said in a mock whisper, "You should let them go to the arcade."

Simon laughed, uttering, "I think I'm out numbered here. The arcade it is!" While Ben and Beckett whooped and hollered, Simon added, "Would you like to join us, Ms. Thorne?"

"Yeah, come with us, Ms. Thorne, please!" Beckett cried, jumping up and down.

"Just be warned, my dad is really, really bad at ski-ball," Ben commented, laughing at his dad's defeated look.

"What do you say?" Simon asked, putting his arms around the boys and making a thumbs-up sign.

Jo laughed and accepted, "Sure, sounds fun." She didn't make a habit out of hanging out with kids and their parents after school. She thought it violated some kind of unwritten rule most of the time. But there were exceptions, and she felt this was one of them.

She wanted the boys to be comfortable with her. She wanted them to know they could come to her with anything, no matter what. She wanted them to be able to trust her, to believe she meant what she said. What better way to do that than with pizza and good old-fashioned arcade games?

"Yes!" cried Beckett. "Come on, come on, I'm starving!" he added, pulling on Simon's arm.

"See you in a few," Jo said, walking back towards the offices to grab her purse and keys.

Simon grabbed Beckett's backpack that was leaning against a locker, voicing, "See you there, Ms. Thorne. Let's go, boys." He waved a goodbye, and they walked down the hall and out the door, thinking of pizza and old arcade games.

* * *

Three months had passed since the incident at school, and things had been pretty good, pretty quiet, as far as Simon was concerned. There had been a couple of times when Vance, Boston, or someone in their group of friends had whispered or laughed when Ben walked by, but for the most part they behaved themselves. They knew the repercussions weren't worth it; at least Simon hoped they knew.

He was surprised at how many students had come forward to offer Ben friendship and support. He nearly teared up when he thought about it. It wasn't that Ben hadn't had friends before; he had. It was just that now the group was different. They had seen true friends stick by Ben's side when things got tough, and they had witnessed kids Ben hadn't hung around much before stand up for him and show their kindness now. It made Simon proud to see these young people being so selfless.

He wasn't as worried as he had been about Ben when he was at school. Simon knew Ben had a good support system there. With Jo, a lot of understanding teachers, and his group of friends, Ben was in good hands. He would still keep his eye on things; of course, he would. But now, for the first time since Olive had left them, he felt like he could let go just a little.

* * *

"What are you thinking, Olive?" Michael asked, all shimmery.

"I feel different now, more free. Like there is less holding me back"—Olive closed her eyes to feel—"I think something happened, Michael. It feels like they don't need me as much as they did before." She felt sad and happy at the same time. She wasn't ready to let go.

"They don't," Michael stated simply.

Olive started to cry. She felt Michael beside her.

"Isn't that what you want, Olive?"

"Yes, but no at the same time." She paused, gathering her thoughts, and then explained, "I want them to be okay, to heal and be able to move on. But, I want them to need me. If they don't need me anymore, they might forget about me. I want them to remember me. I know I sound selfish."

Michael laughed and offered, "You're not selfish, Olive. Your feelings are real, and they matter. But I want you to know that over time it won't matter so much to you if they need you or not. They will always love you, and you know they will never forget you."

Olive loved Michael's laugh. It made something in her heart feel really, really bright, and she felt like he was giving her a big hug. "I know," she replied, "But if they stop needing me, then I won't have a purpose. *They* are my purpose, Michael! I give them what they need, I make sure they are happy! I want them to need me. I don't want that to stop."

"It must stop, Olive, if you want them to move on and live a good life"—Michael was firm—"You have a purpose here, Olive, and when you are ready to see it, you will."

"I'm afraid. What if things happen, and they let me go before I'm ready?" Olive felt scared, she felt weightless in a way she didn't like.

Michael shimmered. He gave her peace, but just a little bit. "It'll be okay," he promised.

7

WITH THINGS WITH BEN MOSTLY BACK ON TRACK, SIMON FELT HE should put more focus on Beckett. On the surface he seemed okay, but Simon wondered what was really going on inside that little head of his.

Thinking some one-on-one time with Beckett might clear things up a bit, Simon was in the middle of sending Mara a text to see if she'd hang out with Ben, so he could take Beckett, when his phone rang. Recognizing it was the school, he picked up right away, hoping Ben was okay.

"Hello?" he answered quickly.

"Hello, Mr. Walker?"

"Yes, this is Simon," he hurriedly replied.

"Hi, this is Jo Thorne, over at the boys' school. We had a little situation with Beckett at recess and were hoping you'd be able to come in, so we can get it all straightened out."

"Situation!" Simon exclaimed, surprised, then checked himself, remembering he was back at work in his office with paper-thin walls. He also didn't want Ms. Thorne to think he was yelling at her. "Sorry, that came out a little . . ." he trailed off, then began again, "What happened? Is Beckett okay?"

"Beckett's okay, he's just upset. He's really wanting his dad right now"— she paused and cleared her throat—"Beckett and a few friends were playing on the monkey bars and somehow the subject of ghosts came up. The kids were talking about who believed in ghosts and why and that sort of thing. Beckett spoke up and told the others a story of how Olive came to visit him with an angel. Some of the kids didn't believe him and told him so, and that's when things escalated."

"Escalated?" Simon questioned, worried.

"Yes, well, some shouting led to more shouting, which lead to a bit of a shoving match. Like I said before, Beckett's okay. The noon supervisor intervened before anyone got hurt, but I think it would be best for him if he had the rest of the day off," Jo explained.

Simon rubbed his temples and sighed into the phone. Would things ever get better, or would this be their life now—putting out one fire, thinking things were good, just to find another one blazing?

"I'll be right in, Ms. Thorne."

"See you soon. Oh, and Mr. Walker? Things will get better, I really believe that. You should too. Just look at how far you've already come," Jo told him before saying goodbye.

He hoped she was right. In a way he knew she was. It was just hard to see right now, in the thick of things. He guessed he was catching onto the boys' schedule and knew all of their favorite snacks for snack time. He knew which school lunches they absolutely would not eat and what was allowed in the cold lunches he packed for them (NO PEANUT BUTTER! But Oreos were okay).

So in that regard, yes, they'd come far, but emotionally? He wasn't so sure.

Simon sent out a quick email letting his team know he'd be taking PTO the rest of the day and quickly shut down his laptop.

Being back at work was easier than Simon had thought it would be. It had helped to get back into the swing of things, and going into the office forced him to get up, take a shower, and get dressed. He had Mara to thank for that. She had been the one to practically push him out the door.

"I can work from home!" he'd insisted, sitting in the office in his three-day old pajamas, hair askew. "It's fine!"

She'd shaken her head and said in a voice she must have used on Olive when she was young, "Get upstairs, get in that shower, and make yourself presentable! You are going into work today, it's time. Now go!"

When he hadn't made a move, she added, "Would you like some help? I've been a mother and a wife for many years, Simon. I'll do it! There's nothing there I haven't seen!"

The look on her face meant business, and Simon didn't doubt her, so he hopped up and hurried up the stairs and into his bathroom. He made sure to lock the door behind him.

When Simon got home that evening, he found Mara at the stove stirring a big pot of spaghetti sauce. "Thank you," he said and meant it, giving her a kiss on the cheek. "I don't know how you knew getting back would be so good for me, but it was."

"You're welcome," she replied smiling at him. "Now go wash your hands. It's almost time for dinner," she issued, as she spun around to face the stove. She didn't want him to see her tearing up. It meant so much for her to see him happy.

On the drive to school Simon thought about what Ms. Thorne had said had happened. Simon knew Beckett was a people pleaser. He wanted everyone to be happy and have fun together. It was important to Beckett that everyone got along. If there was ever an argument, Beckett was the peacemaker.

Simon was surprised that the little guy had gotten into a squabble with any of the other kids. It just wasn't like him. Then again, Simon thought, as he pulled into the school parking lot, when it came to Olive, Beckett was, and always had been, fiercely loyal.

* * *

"I'm sorry, Dad. I'm really, really sorry!" Beckett sobbed in the backseat as Simon put the car in gear and headed towards home.

"It's okay, buddy," Simon replied soothingly, reaching back and patting Beckett on the leg.

"Please don't be mad at me, Daddy. I didn't mean to get into trouble," Beckett wailed.

"I'm not mad, Beckett. It's okay." Simon tried to sound convincing, but inside he was seething.

"You look mad, Dad. You look *really* mad! You look like the mean guy on Lego Batman!" Beckett sniffed.

"Gee, thanks," Simon muttered under his breath, then deciding to make a short detour, took his next right and pulled into the Dairy Queen parking lot. He unbuckled his seatbelt and turned around to face Beckett, whose face was still red and tear-stained. "I'm not mad at you, but I am a little mad at the kids from school. I'm also kind of upset with some of the teachers at school."

Beckett's lip started to quiver and the tears started flowing again. "I'm sorry!" he cried.

Looking at Beckett's heartbroken face, Simon felt like he wanted to cry too, and for a second he almost let himself. Reminding himself that he was the parent, he contorted his body, somehow squeezing it into the backseat next to Beckett. Telling himself he didn't want to go through the embarrassment of some unsuspecting person walking by and seeing a child and a grown man sobbing together in a car in the Dairy Queen parking lot, he bit his lip and pulled Beckett into a big hug.

"You did nothing wrong, buddy. You did nothing wrong. I'm not mad at you, and I promise that I will get over being mad at all the kids and teachers in a little bit. I just need to think about all that happened and work it out. I just need to process it all, okay?" Simon rubbed Beckett's back and breathed in his sweet little-boy scent until he was calmed down.

"What does 'process it all' mean, Dad?" Beckett asked, looking up at him with his innocent eyes.

"It means I need to let my brain think about it. When something is bothering me, I just need to think about it for a while and then decide it's going to be okay. After I decide it's going to be okay, then I can let it go and not be upset about it anymore," Simon explained as he smiled down at Beckett and wiped away a few stray tears.

Beckett nodded and commented, "That's what Ben does too. So you and Ben are the same like that and me and Mom are the same in how we are. We like to talk about it, and then we decide we want to be happy, so we try to let it go too."

Simon smiled at Beckett, wondering how he ever got to be so brilliant. Then he frowned as Beckett's face darkened.

"It's not fair, Dad. I wasn't lying about Mom coming to visit me with an angel. She did! She came to me, and she came to Ben and so did her angel. His name is Michael, and it's true!" Beckett exclaimed.

"I know, Beckett, and I believe you, but not everyone believes in that kind of stuff," Simon told him simply.

"Why, Dad?" Beckett asked, hurt.

"Well, a lot of grown-ups think that kind of stuff is make-believe, and that's what they tell their kids. Some people have a hard time believing in something that they can't see. To them you have to see it to believe it. People who believe that way will have a very hard time believing in what you were talking about. I think sometimes people are afraid to believe in what they can't see because they don't understand it. They don't know what it is or what it means. They can't explain it and that makes them uncomfortable."

Beckett chewed on his lip thoughtfully for a while and then asked, "Do you think anyone believes me?"

Simon's heart broke a little bit at his son's hopeful expression. He so badly wanted to share the experience he'd had with his mom with everyone, but unfortunately, it wasn't something that was allowed to be shared at show-and-tell anymore. "I don't know, bud. I bet there are some people who believe you, or want to believe you, or who would really like to hear your story. The trick is to figure out the best time and place to talk about it, right?"

Beckett nodded, looking glum.

"From now on, we can talk about it at home as much as you want. Which is the best place anyway, because then you and Ben can talk about it together since you both know all about it. But, at school we should try not to talk about it, okay?" Simon hated himself for having this conversation with Beckett, but he knew he needed to. He didn't think it was fair to tell his children when they could or couldn't talk about their mom, but the principal was clear when he had picked Beckett up that afternoon. Talking about Olive in that *capacity*, was *off limits on school property*. Too many teachers were already complaining, worried they would have angry parents on their hands. Anything religious was off limits.

"But it's not *religious*! It's not even *about religion*!" Simon had protested. "*Freedom of speech!*" he had wanted to shout but had decided it wasn't the best idea.

"Again, Mr. Walker," the principal had sighed loudly, leaning so far back in his chair he almost toppled over, "we just can't have that kind of talk circulating the school. Too many angry, uncomfortable parents. Too many kids asking too many questions that we here at public school just don't have the ability to answer."

Simon had bit his tongue and done his best not to flip the old geezer the bird as he walked out with a sobbing Beckett in tow.

"I'm sorry, buddy. If I had it my way, you could talk about it whenever, but that's just not the way things are right now." Simon gave Beckett a half smile.

"Okay, Dad. But it's not fair, it's just not fair," Beckett mumbled.

"I know, bud. I know," Simon agreed, "Well, should we go on in and get some ice cream for later tonight? I'm pretty sure Gizzy's making beef stew tonight, and I think Butterfinger Blizzards would be the perfect thing for dessert."

"Yeah!" Beckett cried happily, the incident forgotten for the moment. "Do you think I can get something for before dinner? Maybe a Star Kiss or something?" he asked, smiling up adoringly at Simon.

"I think that could be arranged," Simon replied, his heart lightening at Beckett's smile. "You know," he continued as they got out of the car and started across the parking lot, "I bet someday people will be begging you to tell the story of how Mom visited you with her angel."

"Really?" Beckett asked, eyes round and bright, as he bounced into the building next to Simon.

"I think so," Simon told him with a smile, "It's a special story and you're a special guy, Beckett. Always remember that. Got it?"

"Got it!" Beckett cried as he ran to the freezer and sorted through the red Star Kisses, finding the perfect one.

* * *

Olive looked down at Simon and Beckett and smiled. "I'm so proud of them," she remarked.

Michael laughed, agreeing, "I know."

"What so funny?" Olive questioned.

He shimmered as he revealed, "You're glowing."

Olive looked at herself. She did seem to be a little sparkly. She felt another one of her ties to her family and her old life loosen and give way completely. "It happened again, Michael. I feel lighter, like I'm not as tied to them as I was before."

"It's almost time, Olive," Michael noted quietly.

"Time for what?"

"For you to discover what it is you came here to do. Your plan," Michael replied, gauging her reaction.

She waited for a moment to respond, waited for him to give her peace, but he didn't. She thought about what he'd said and wondered why she didn't feel as upset or afraid as she had before. Thinking about leaving her family and moving on to something else still hurt her heart. She still wasn't ready. But she didn't feel the profound sadness that she had before. What she felt was more like an acceptance and realization that things really were going to be okay.

There was a split second where she worried that maybe there was something wrong with her, that she should be missing them more. Holding tight to them and not ever letting go.

Then Michael nudged her from the inside, reassuring her, *You're right where you need to be.*

She jumped, still not used to him not having to actually speak to her. "There is a part of me that knows that what you are saying is real and true, deep down I *know* this, I *feel* this. But there is another part of me that wants to fight and scream and claw myself back to them. How do I let go of that part of me? I know that I need to, and I am beginning to want to. I just don't know if I can; it still feels so much like I'm giving up on them."

"You need to accept and acknowledge those feelings. Know that all of what you are feeling is okay to feel. Let go of the judgment and let in the love. When you accept that part of yourself completely, that part of you will fall away. Then you will be ready to move on," explained Michael.

"Okay," she said, thinking about what he had told her. She knew what he said was true, she just wasn't sure how she was going to get there. She wondered if he used his voice to explain it to her or if he used his thoughts; it was getting more difficult as time went on to tell the difference.

Michael laughed, and Olive felt herself brighten.

"You'll get used to it," he offered.

"Promise?" she asked, uncertainly.

"I do," he said and gave her peace. But just a little.

8

SIMON WAS MAD AT OLIVE. HE WAS FURIOUS. HE FELT GUILTY FOR BE-ing so upset at someone that was dead, but not bad enough to pull himself out of it.

How could she go and leave them like this? How could she have been so thoughtless to cross the street without looking both ways? She was constantly on the boys for doing just that, but she hadn't listened to her own rule, and look what it had cost them!

The boys were at school, and Simon was working from home though he would admit he wasn't getting much work done. He sat stewing in his office, thinking about Olive's careless mistake while biting the heck out of the cap of a pen.

Mara had picked up on his foul mood after breakfast that morning, and she'd made a quick exit after the boys had gotten on the bus, hoping some time alone would help clear his mind. However, when she returned a few hours later to see him sitting exactly where he had been when she left, foul mood still intact, she figured she'd have to intervene.

"Well, I see your mood hasn't improved," she commented as she sat down on one of the chairs in the office, opposite Simon's desk.

"What do you mean?" Simon grunted, shifting in his chair as he moved the pen cap to the other side of his mouth.

"You're still irritable, and it doesn't take much to see you haven't done anything besides sit there and work yourself up into a state. The only thing that has changed since this morning is that pen cap. That *is* a pen cap, right?"

Mara made a face as Simon removed the now unrecognizable pen cap from his mouth and tossed it into the trash. "Yeah, well, being mad at Olive doesn't seem to be conducive to getting any work done."

Mara looked at Simon with a raised eyebrow and waited for him to con-tinue.

"I'm so *mad* at her, Mara. I'm mad that she left us. I'm mad that she was dumb enough to cross the street and get hit by a car. I'm mad that she's not here to help with the boys. I'm mad that everything falls to me now, no matter what. How am I supposed to shoulder all of that? How could she do this to us?" Simon took a deep breath, let it out and added, "I'm sorry. She was your daughter. I shouldn't be saying this to you."

"She was your wife," Mara replied, "And, yes, you should. Who else would you say it to?"

"I don't know. Nobody probably," Simon answered as he leaned forward and rested his forehead in his hands.

"Being upset with her doesn't make you a bad person, Simon. It makes you normal." When he didn't respond, she continued, "I was mad at her too, you know." Mara smiled as Simon looked up at her, surprised. "I was. A few weeks ago. I was so angry with her, for leaving you and the boys. For leaving *me*. I worked myself up over it, so much so that I started yelling at her. I yelled and yelled and yelled. I told her everything I was thinking."

Simon shook his head, "I don't think so. I would have heard that."

"It was one of your first days back at work, and the boys were at school. I had the whole place to myself," Mara disclosed as she spread her arms wide. "Oh boy, did it feel great. Until it didn't. Believe me, most of what I said was not very nice. I felt horrible after that, thinking of all I yelled out to my deceased daughter. I beat myself up about it too, until I remembered that I'd done the same thing after Olive's father died."

Simon sat up in his chair, looking intrigued.

"Oh, I was so mad at him," Mara reminisced. "After Olive left with a couple of friends to go to the pool, I started to yell. I think I yelled at him half the day. I probably would have kept going too, but I noticed the kitchen window was open and didn't want to scare the neighborhood kids any more than I already had"—Mara laughed at the memory—"A couple of minutes later my doorbell rang. It was one of the young stay-at-home moms from down the street. She had lost her husband about six months prior. She had heard me yelling and wanted to let me know that it was okay, it was normal to be upset. She said that she had felt so guilty about how mad she had been at her husband when he died that she had fallen into a deep depression. She had beaten herself up about it every day and beaten herself up about not being a good mom and on and on, until she finally made herself go to a grief support group. That day the group had been talking about anger, of all things. She said that night she had gone home and cried and cried and cried, not because she missed her husband, or because she was angry with him. But because she finally understood that it was normal and okay to feel how she was feeling towards her dearly departed husband. The point is"—Mara smiled at Simon—"that when you accept how you feel and don't try to fight it or tell yourself it's wrong, the easier it is to move on. The easier it is to heal. We're human, we're going to have feelings toward Olive that aren't always nice and kind. We just need to remind ourselves that it's okay. And as for everything falling onto your shoulders, you know I am here for you. I am your partner now, no matter how silly it might sound, I am. I'll be here until you no longer need me, and then I'll still be here because it's always nice to have somebody."

Simon let out a quiet laugh, confiding, "Believe it or not, that actually makes me feel better. But ... if this is your way of trying to talk me into going to some grief group, I'm going to have to give you a big, resounding NO."

Mara chuckled, admitting, "I'm not much of a grief group person either. To each his own, right? You and me—we can be our own group." She stood up slowly, stretching her legs. "Alright, I'll leave you to it. The boys are going to be home in about an hour," she noted, checking her watch.

"Oh, crap," Simon muttered under his breath, wondering how he was going to jam eight hours of work into one measly hour.

"Language!" joked Mara as she walked down the hall to the guest room, thinking of how nice a catnap sounded. She was happy she was retired.

* * *

It started with a sound, barely perceptible, but there nonetheless. It wasn't the way Olive had thought it would start. She had pictured something more obvious. Louder and more clear. Looking back though, it made sense. If it had been any different, all the pieces wouldn't have fallen into place in such a perfect way.

"What's that?" Olive asked with a start. She had been buzzing around with Michael, enjoying the new feeling of not being in the form of her body.

She'd been afraid at first when she'd noticed it wasn't there, but Michael had encouraged her to give it a try, and she'd slowly warmed to the feeling.

"You can always go back to your body form if you'd like," Michael had told her, "but try not being in form for a while. You're showing me you're ready to try it, Olive. Otherwise you wouldn't have shifted out of form in the first place." He smiled knowingly at her and added, "Just for a little bit, and then you can go back into form."

She'd trusted him and was surprised at how natural it felt to not be in body form. She felt free and light, like she imagined it would feel to be a bright white cloud. She wasn't ready to give up her body form completely though, promising Michael she would continue to try being without it more and more often. There was something inside of her holding her back from letting go of her body form. She knew once she let it go, that was it, no going back, and though she accepted that soon she would have to let it go, she was still attached to it. It reminded her of her family, and though she knew it was silly to think it, part of her still believed that letting her body form go would mean letting her family go too. She needed to get past that attachment, needed to be more rooted in the belief that her body form was just a kind of manifestation for her, and that being without it wouldn't hinder her. She could feel that belief growing slowly and knew deep down that soon she'd be ready. Just not yet.

"Do you hear that?" she asked Michael again, coming back into body form and tilting her head to the side.

Michael sparkled at her as she was drawn towards the sound.

"I think someone's crying," she said, concerned, "It sounds like a child. Do you hear it, Michael?"

"Yes. Do you see?" Michael asked, pointing towards a young boy who was sitting underneath a big oak tree.

He hadn't needed to point it out to her though. It was almost as if she had seen it before he had. She could feel the pain and sorrow surrounding the small boy, and she rushed to his side to help. "What's wrong, sweetheart?" she asked, kneeling down beside him.

"I'm scared," he blubbered between sobs. "I don't know where I am, and look," he said, pointing, "My mom and dad are crying. I tried to talk to them and ask them what's wrong, but they didn't hear me. They were scared last night too, when we had to go to the hospital, but I told them I was going to be okay and I am, see! I told them I wasn't sick, and I'm not! Why won't they listen to me? Who are you?" He looked up at Olive and wiped his eyes.

Olive felt Michael beside her and was relieved. She felt paralyzed at the idea of having to tell this sweet young boy that he had passed away. That the reason his parents couldn't hear him was because he wasn't there anymore. She wished she knew the perfect thing to say. Had magic words to heal him in an instant.

"Let me show you," she heard Michael whisper to her, "Pay attention, this is important." She felt the words as if he had pressed them into her heart.

"Hello," he said gently, and Olive saw him give the boy peace, "I'm Michael. I have something to tell you, but you're going to have to be really, really brave. Do you think you can do that?"

The boy nodded solemnly, and Olive felt her heart break into pieces once more. She closed her eyes. When she opened them, she was surprised to see a light. Barely shining, it surrounded the boy with what Olive felt was pure love. The light gave her hope that everything was going to be okay, and she felt peace.

The longer Olive looked at the light, the more she was filled with a knowing that this hope and peace could come from her too. She began to feel a sense of purpose growing within herself, and she thought back to when He had shown her the plan. She couldn't read it then, hadn't wanted to, but now she could see a part of it. Little by little, it was taking shape.

9

WHEN SIMON WOKE AND CHECKED HIS PHONE THAT MORNING, HE WAS startled as he noticed the date displayed on the screen. It was exactly six months to the day since Olive's accident.

Christmas had come and gone, and they had gotten through it. Albeit with a large amount of Kleenex, heartache, and a distracting amount of presents to keep the boys' spirits up. And Mara, thank god for Mara, she'd been the one to whisk them off to and fro—hot chocolates and Christmas parades, Christmas music, a driving tour of the best-lit neighborhoods in the city, *Scrooge* at the children's theater, and more.

So, yes, they had gotten through it, but barely. It had been devastating to see the boys come down the stairs on Christmas morning, both so fiercely wishing for their mom, but having to face the heartbreaking reality that she would never be there again. There were no excited screams over presents and checking to see if Santa had come. There were only subdued smiles and half-hearted cheer.

Oh, how Simon had wished they'd woken him at the crack of dawn and forced him to stumble down the stairs to watch them open presents before he'd even had a sip of coffee. Would he ever hear their voices filled with joy on Christmas again, or was this how it was going to be from now on? If it was, he'd take it, he had no choice, but he kind of hated himself in that moment. He wished he would have paid more attention all the Christmases before and enjoyed the time they'd had together.

It was funny how time changed things, how something that seemed painful a year ago could be the one thing you wished for now. How sometimes you wished the normal routine could be different, but when it changed, all you could think about was how great normal had been.

Simon had wished and wished for what he considered normal, at Christmas, all along knowing that things had changed. Olive's absence had been especially devastating to each one of them during the holidays, and though it was beyond difficult for Simon to accept that Olive would never share those moments with them again, he knew he had to. For the sake of himself and his boys, Simon was determined to bring the joy back to his family.

He double-checked the date, barely believing it really had been six months. It was one of those moments, where upon reflection, it seemed that time had passed in the blink of an eye, but also as if moving through thick molasses.

He wasn't sure how long ago the barrage of visitors and friends calling to check in had stopped. It had to have been a few months, at least. It seemed odd to him that he hadn't noticed people had stopped coming around. He supposed they had slowly stopped calling, stopped coming, when they noticed he at least appeared to be surviving. Or maybe he had driven them away with his lack of wanting to really connect?

He wasn't sure. He had been a walking zombie for months after Olive had died, so thank goodness for Mara, always making sure things were running smoothly. *It couldn't have been easy for her either*, Simon thought, *but she'd done it*. She'd answered the door and phone. Welcomed in anyone who ventured by, reassuring them it was okay they had stopped by and to "please come in." Listened gratefully when someone wanted to share a memory of Olive. She seemed to know that others needed to grieve as well, that they needed to connect with someone who had known Olive. Needed to talk about her.

Simon had dreaded those moments, and if he could get away with it, he'd sit in his office "working" or would hide upstairs in either Beckett's or Ben's room. He had gotten his fill of Legos and Wii those first few months but had known the time he spent with his boys wasn't replaceable.

He knew he should have made more of an effort when visitors came or called, but it had been too difficult for him. He hadn't wanted to break down in front of friends or acquaintances. That would have been awkward and uncomfortable for everyone involved. He hadn't been ready. But now, he thought, he was. The next time someone stopped by or called, he'd answer. He hoped they'd understand.

After Simon took a shower and got dressed, he made his way downstairs and poured himself a cup of coffee. It was Friday and for the past couple months he had made a point to work from home on Fridays. It was a nice relaxing way to end the workweek and start up the weekend.

The boys had been so happy they had started calling it "Fun Friday." Simon had taken it a step farther and had started coming up with fun things for them to do on Friday nights. Usually they ordered pizza and watched a movie on Netflix, but sometimes they went to Saucy Baby (best arcade ever!), bowling, or mini golfing. A couple of times they had gotten tickets to see a Wild's game. Simon had always loved hockey. It was fun to have a new tradition for him and the boys, but it sometimes made him miss Olive even more. She would have loved Fun Fridays.

Sitting down in front of his laptop, Simon heard his phone ding. He pulled it out of his pocket, hoping he hadn't missed a call from the school. It was funny how much he cared about his missed calls now that Olive was gone. It hadn't bothered him much before because there wasn't much he had to worry about that would need his immediate attention—besides his work, but even that was rarely an emergency. If something had happened with the boys, he'd known Olive would be there and find a way to let him know she needed him, if she did. Now, though, he was always worried he'd miss a call from school about one of the boys being sick or hurt or who knows what. He always said a quick little prayer when the phone rang, that it wouldn't be the school.

Glancing down at his phone, he saw he had a reminder about Ben's IEP meeting next week. Simon leaned back in his chair and sighed. This had always been Olive's department. She had been the one to go to all the school meetings and figure out just what Ben needed to make him successful. Simon hadn't. He didn't know all of what Olive knew. He had been involved, of course, but he would listen as Olive reported back what had happened at the meetings, laughing or shaking his head at some of the things that were said, but that had been the extent of it. If Olive asked him his opinion, he told her what he thought, but ultimately it was up to her to decide what action to take because she had all of the information. She knew it all backwards and forwards.

Hindsight being 20/20, he now saw he should have been more involved in the process, but at the time it hadn't seemed necessary. It wasn't that he didn't care; he did. It was just simpler for Olive to take care of everything. Olive hadn't minded either; it was easier for her to know that if a decision needed to be made, she could go ahead and make it without having to discuss it with Simon. They both wanted the same thing for Ben, so to them it had been simple. Until it wasn't.

He supposed he had no choice but to move forward. Even though he felt as if he'd be going in blind, he would do his best for Ben. He wondered if Ms. Thorne would be there. She worked with Ben on a weekly basis, so it would make sense that she would be there. Wouldn't it? He shot her a quick email. If she could be there, he wouldn't feel so lost. He wouldn't feel so alone.

Before settling back into his work, it struck him again that while it had been six months since Olive's passing, it had been going well, all things considered.

The boys were gradually getting back to their old selves. The consistency of good days were slowly beginning to outweigh the bad. They still had their bad days though, and getting through them was nothing less than heartbreaking.

There were times when something exciting would happen, and one of the boys would shout, "I can't wait to tell Mom!" before their reality caught up with them. Simon had picked up the phone more times than he could remember to call Olive, only to have the memory of her death rush up to greet him as his finger hovered over her name on his phone.

Life can be cruel, Simon thought, *how your mind can play tricks on you, giving you hope and then ripping it away the moment you needed it the most.* Simon knew life could be beautiful too, and he tried keeping that in mind as much as he tried to stay strong for his boys, but it was hard. Soul-crushingly hard.

Even with their good-day streaks lasting longer and longer, when a bad day hit, he felt like he was being sucked into the eye of the storm. It was all he could do sometimes to hold it together until the boys were tucked safely into their beds, asleep. When he was sure they were asleep, he'd fall into bed, his body shaking as he sobbed into his pillow. Would it ever get better, really better? He read it would, had been told it would, but he wasn't sure. Sometimes, on those dark days, he could feel his hope slipping away, being replaced by a sorrow so deep and dark that Simon thought he might never escape it.

* * *

"He's still hurting. He needs me, and so do the boys. How can I leave them? How can I make that my choice when they still have so far to go before they are healed?" asked Olive, all the while feeling tears running down her cheeks and realizing she had gone back into body form.

She rarely was in body form anymore. It was easier to not be, and she was beginning to like it better. She liked the way being free of form felt. Lighter, less held down. It became obvious to her now that the only times she went back to body form were when she was thinking of her family or when she got overly emotional. She realized her body was like her crutch; when she felt upset or saddened by what was happening with her family, her body comforted her.

She also realized those feelings of fear and deep sadness were directly tied to her physical life. She knew that when she was ready to move on, those feelings would disappear with her body, leaving only pure love, joy, and happiness in their wake. That's how things were here. Made of love and kindness. Everything made sense because you could see the entire plan playing out in front of you, so there was no reason *to* be sad. It was all beautiful, in its own way. You just had to be ready to accept it and want to change.

"It's all in your mind," Michael reminded her, sparkling, "When you change the way you look at things, everything starts to change."

Olive wiped her eyes and looked at Michael, surprising herself with the realization that he wasn't so bright and sparkly as he had been when she'd first seen him.

He laughed, explaining, "It's because you're becoming bright and sparkly too." He touched her cheek and continued, "There is a reason you're here, Olive. To comfort others who have passed. To help them understand what you now understand, to see things as you are now beginning to see them. It's your choice to decide when you are fully ready for what you came here to do, but as you can see, it has already started." He gestured to the small boy slowly climbing up the big oak tree.

The boy could feel their eyes on him, so he looked over and waved, exclaiming, "Look at me, Olive! Look how high I am! I can even see my mom and dad from here!" He laughed as he looked down on them, and Olive saw the laughter sparkle and shine and fall like raindrops onto his parents, helping them heal just a little bit more.

Olive felt her heart fill with love, and her body fell away. She loved that little boy, loved him with a fierceness that surprised her because he wasn't hers. She had only ever felt that way towards Beckett and Ben.

The thought that popped into her mind first was that she shouldn't feel this way, that it wasn't fair for her boys. But that thought didn't feel right; it felt wrong and filled with fear. Olive could feel her body form coming back, but she didn't want it or need it right now. She knew deep within that loving this boy didn't diminish her love for Beckett and Ben; it only added to it. Every time she looked at this boy, her heart grew a little bit bigger, shone a little bit brighter, just like it did when she looked at her own sons.

She saw now how things were connected, how what she did could affect more people than she had first thought. The more love she had inside, the more she could give. When she gave love to this new little boy, he began to heal, and when he began to heal, he began to give love in the form of happiness to his parents. The happiness he gave to his parents helped them heal. When they healed, they could move on and give love to another little boy or girl that might come to them in the future. So, no, loving someone who wasn't her child, who wasn't part of her, wouldn't take away from anything. In fact, the opposite was true. The more love she gave, the more there was to go around. Olive realized this as she watched the little boy gaze down on his parents. *That's what everyone should do,* she thought, looking down and noticing for the first time how everyone was connected, *Love each other. Just love each other.*

Michael smiled, laughed, shimmered. She felt his love for her radiating out so strongly that she had to close her eyes and take a deep breath. It was a love so profound that it almost hurt. It was so, so beautiful.

"When you first got here, He said you were a lovely example of what a mother's love is like. Do you remember that?" Michael asked.

"Yes," Olive replied, "But why does that matter?"

"It's important you remember that. Your purpose here is great. What you will do is important. In the beginning, even after you fully accept, it can be hard. Emotions can leak through, and you might question yourself. In those moments, remember what He said. Remember this, I believe in you, Olive." Michael shimmered and then gave her peace because he wanted to.

"Why do I feel like you're saying goodbye?" Olive asked. She felt worry settling in, but just as quickly as the feeling came, it was gone.

"I'm not," Michael answered simply, "Soon though, it will be time for you to decide if you accept your purpose. Then you will need to say goodbye to your family, and I will continue on my path as you continue on yours."

"What if I need you?" Olive questioned.

"You'll just need to think of me, and I'll be here. But I doubt you'll need me," explained Michael with a smile.

"How can you have so much confidence in me?" Olive marveled.

Michael shimmered, "Because I can see the plan from here, and I love you. I know what you can do, and I believe in you."

Olive took a breath, thinking of what he said, and then admitted, "I don't think I'll ever be ready to say goodbye to my family."

Michael placed his hand on her shoulder and offered, "It's not truly goodbye, Olive. You'll still be able to look in on them. Visit them once in a while. You'll just be shifting your focus, paying more attention to what's in front of you instead of behind."

"How much time do I have?" Olive asked, thinking of how she'd miss her family. Of how she'd miss this time with Michael.

He smiled at her, shimmered just a little, and she knew the answer without even having to hear it.

* * *

Surprisingly, Ben's IEP meeting went off without a hitch. Or maybe it wasn't so surprising, Simon mused, as he thought about what had happened.

The morning of the meeting, Simon readied himself as best he could. Mara was with the boys, and would be getting them on the bus.

The night before, Mara had quietly brought up the subject of her moving back home. It had been an emotionally draining discussion for both of them, but they agreed it had to happen. Simon knew it was only a matter of time before she'd be gone for good. Though it wouldn't really be so bad. She was only an hour away and could be there if they needed her in a heartbeat. Although he still felt a little uneasy about it, Simon knew it was about time to start getting things back to normal, and that included Mara being back at her own place. It was important for them all to prove it to themselves that they could do it on their own.

Checking his phone for a second time, Simon walked into the family room to give each boy a hug goodbye. They were back to playing Mario Kart, and though Olive hadn't let them play electronics in the mornings, Simon sometimes let it slide. It was good to see them happy.

Beckett gave Simon a quick squeeze, more worried about his brother beating him at the game than where his dad was going. His actions didn't go unnoticed by Simon, acknowledging that only a few short months ago Beckett wouldn't let his dad leave his side. Simon's heart swelled, realizing they were making progress.

"Bye, Dad, love you," Ben uttered as he hugged his dad tight, then added, "I've been doing my best, Dad, and I think it's been really good. I'm in a book club now with other kids from class, not the one I was in at the beginning of the year. You know, the one where I had to leave class to go to? And math's still hard, but not as bad."

Simon smiled, wishing Olive could see Ben now. "I'm so proud of you, Ben."

Ben nodded, but his attention was back on the game now.

Simon walked into the kitchen and grabbed his keys from Mara's outstretched hand, "Thanks again Mara. I hope this goes okay. You know I have no idea what to do, right?" he declared anxiously.

Mara laughed, assuring him, "You're going to be fine. From what I gathered from what Olive said before, you really just sit there while they go over Ben's progress. Then at the end you can ask questions"—she laughed again at the look on his face—"You've got this, Simon." She pushed him out the door, calling, "Good luck!"

When Simon arrived at the school and pulled his car into a parking spot, his heart was beating triple time. He had no idea when the last time was he'd been so nervous. He took a deep breath and thought of Olive. Of all the times she'd done what he was doing right now. Had she been nervous? He didn't think so, but if she had, she'd gone in there and taken care of business anyway.

"Olive," he stated, his voice cracking. He wasn't sure if she could hear him, but even if she couldn't, the thought of talking to her comforted him, so he continued, "Olive, I wish you were here with me. Then you could tell me what to do, what to say. I don't want to mess this up. You were Ben's warrior, but you're not here anymore, so it falls to me"—he paused, sighed, kept going—"I feel so ill-equipped for the job, but I'm the only one who can do it, so I promise you, I'm going to do my best. If you can hear me, if you are listening, then please just give me some type of sign in there, so I *know* that I'm doing the right thing. I don't care what it is, a butterfly flying by or someone sneezing three times in a row like you used to, anything." He took a couple deep, calming breaths—a technique he would have laughed at before—and got out of this car.

The first face Simon saw as he entered the meeting room was of Ms. Thorne, and he was immediately put at ease. She was the only one in the room, and she smiled at him as he took a seat across the table from her.

"Thank god," he commented quietly, "I thought I might have to go this alone. I wasn't sure what was going to happen if that was the case. Thank you for being here." He looked around the room, at the oblong table, closely crowded with chairs waiting to be filled, and thought of Olive. He wondered how she had felt the first time she'd sat down in this room—had she been as nervous as he was? He supposed she had told him all about it, but he couldn't remember now. He wished she were here.

Ms. Thorne laughed quietly, telling him, "You're welcome. Because I work with Ben a few times a week, I was already planning on coming before you emailed me, but I'm happy you want me here. Oh, and don't for a minute think you are in this alone, Simon. We all want what's best for Ben, and I have a list of things written down that Olive and I spoke about earlier this year, so—"

It was at this moment, as the other teachers were walking in, that Jo Thorne sneezed three times in a row, leaving Simon speechless.

"Bless you, Jo!" declared a teacher Simon hadn't seen before, as she sat down.

"Oh, thank you," Jo responded, blushing, "I don't know where that came from. I rarely sneeze, and never three times in a row!" She laughed.

"Alright, let's get started, shall we?" the principal asked the group, looking at Simon for the go-ahead.

Simon could barely nod his head in agreement. His heart was beating hard against his chest. He'd asked for a sign and he'd gotten it; he could hardly believe it. If he paid attention to only one person in the meeting, that person would definitely be Ms. Thorne.

As the meeting went on, Simon could barely believe what he was hearing. "Ben is doing great! He has been excelling in reading! He is now in one of the highest-level book clubs in his grade! Everyone has been amazed at his progress! He is a hard worker and determined, and those skills will serve him well in life," shared one teacher. Simon agreed, his heart soaring. Math still needed work, but he was getting it!

He no longer needed reading intervention. He no longer needed someone to read to him the words on the tests he took to make sure he could understand! He could have someone read it to him if he chose, but it was his choice. He was great at typing! He was going to have an accommodation added so that he could type out his homework/notes/test answers that needed to be in paragraph form. He was getting an iPad, so he could use that to take pictures of his daily homework.

His handwriting still needed work, it was messy, and even Ben couldn't always read what he'd written. "In this situation iPads have worked well," a teacher explained, "We don't want Ben getting frustrated because he can't read his writing. We don't want him missing homework or getting an answer wrong on a test because the teacher can't read it either. An iPad can help with that. Was Simon okay with that?"

Simon wondered whether Ben getting an iPad might be a hindrance because then he'd never have to write anything.

"An iPad will help Ben not become frustrated with his writing, especially when he has a lot to write or is in a hurry," Ms. Thorne offered, "He will still work on his handwriting because he gets pulled out of class especially for that. If he has an iPad, he might be more willing to work hard during the time he gets pulled for handwriting because he won't have to write more when he gets back to class."

Ben got pulled out of class to work on handwriting? This was news to Simon. Confused he questioned, "Why does Ben need to get pulled from class?"

"A lot of children who are dyslexic have a hard time with writing. Ben is not lazy. It is just really hard for him and his hand gets tired easily," the handwriting teacher explained, "He pushes down extremely hard when he is writing, and that takes a lot of energy. We are working on that. We are working on writing slowly, neatly. He is doing a great job, but we've noticed when he can type things out in the classroom, he is more apt to do a better job and stay focused on his handwriting during that specific time."

Simon nodded, confirming, "That makes sense, and yes to the iPad!"

The meeting flew by and when it is over Simon was left with a sense of hope and peace when he thought about Ben. There was a time when thinking about Ben and his struggles in school left Simon feeling hopeless and full of sorrow. He remembered at the beginning, when Ben was first starting to struggle, how Simon had no idea what to do. He felt like a failure because up until that point, whenever there was something going wrong, he'd known just what to do to fix it.

He remembered the months of waiting to figure out what was going on with his perfect little boy. All the testing they'd taken him to do, all the questionnaires they'd had to fill out. He didn't know how many times he'd had to answer the question, "Does your child act as if moved by a robot?" He'd had no idea what that even meant! So he'd had come to the conclusion that Ben didn't "act as if moved by a robot," because if he did, then Simon would surely have understand that question.

He remembered when they'd finally gotten a diagnosis, dyslexia. He had never liked to label things and hadn't wanted to label his son, never would, but putting a name to the cause of what they had been going through had made Simon feel a little bit better. He'd felt like a weight had been lifted off his shoulders; he'd felt that there just might be hope.

He remembered Olive. She had worried and worried and worried and worried for weeks, no months, on end. She'd been the most emotional he had ever seen her, and that was saying a lot. She'd hated the fact that they'd had to put Ben through so much testing. She'd hated filling out questionnaires that made their son seem less of a person and more of a thing to be fixed. She'd hated the fact that he had been struggling in school for so long before they'd been able to get him help.

Ben had started to have anxiety about school. He had started yelling at them when they were trying to help him with his homework, screaming, "I'm stupid!" over and over again. He'd been shutting down at school also, crying at random times. Olive had blamed herself for his anxiety. She had beaten herself up over the fact that she hadn't seen his sadness sooner. She'd felt that other parents were judging her because her son was different, and sometimes she'd wanted to smack the kids that were being mean to Ben.

Simon had been surprised at her latter admission, but secretly he'd felt the same way. He hadn't understood how kids could be so mean at such a young age. It had hurt him deeply to see Ben hurting, to see Olive hurting. Besides what he had been going through now—losing Olive and having to move on with his life without her, figuring out what had been going on with Ben—supporting Ben with his learning differences had been the most difficult thing he had ever done.

So when they had finally gotten a diagnosis, finally started to get him help at school, the relief that they felt caused them both to break down in tears. They were finally able to let go of the stress and anxiety and fear of the unknown and move forward towards what they had hoped would be success.

"You're going to have to celebrate his success tonight. He's done an amazing job over these past few months" Ms. Thorne remarked, cutting into Simon's thoughts and bringing him back into the present moment.

Looking around the meeting table, Simon saw the proud, smiling faces of all the teachers that had helped Ben along the way. The principal was there too, and though Simon wasn't a huge fan because of what had happened with Beckett and the angel talk, Simon could tell that he was just as proud as everyone else in the room. The comments the principal had made about Ben had been kind and supportive, and Simon thought that maybe he'd been too quick to jump to conclusions before.

Deciding to give the guy another shot, Simon smiled and made eye contact with each person in the room, declaring, "Thank you all so much for the work you've done with Ben. It means a lot to me, and I know it would mean a lot to Olive"—he stopped for a moment, to catch his breath; he didn't want to get choked up at his first school meeting—"It has been hard with Olive gone. I'm the first one to admit that I've had a lot to learn. Picking up her slack hasn't been easy, and that's because she was so amazing at what she did. I've been doing my best, but even then I can only hope to be half as good as she was with the kids. I appreciate the support and patience you've given Ben, and even Beckett"—Simon looked at Ms. Thorne and smiled—"Things have been starting to get a little easier, and now . . . hearing this, well, it just makes me so proud."

There was a lot of sniffing and clearing of throats until the principal spoke up, "I think I can speak for everyone when I say that we are all so very proud of Ben as well. He is such a hard worker and a genuinely good kid"— the teachers around the table nodded in agreement—"We are all so very sorry for your loss, Simon. Olive was well liked by the students and staff here, and we all miss her dearly. I can't imagine what it must be like for you and your boys. I hope you know we are here for you. We support you and are also proud of the progress you three have made as a family. You are doing a great job getting them through this, Simon, I hope you know that."

Simon nodded. It was almost too much to take in. He was surprised at how supported he felt. He had thought that they would be impatient with him, annoyed that he hadn't put in as much effort as Olive had. Frustrated that they had to repeat things that everyone else knew inside and out, but that wasn't the case.

He no longer felt alone in the whole Ben school area. He could tell these people honestly cared about his son and his family, and wanted to do what they could to help. This meant a lot to him, surprisingly more than he'd have expected, and it took him a while to collect himself.

Sensing this, the principal came over and patted Simon gently on the back, then left. The others followed suit until there were only Simon and Ms. Thorne in the room.

"You okay?" she asked lightly.

Trying to compose himself, he took a deep breath in and then let it out. Finally, he responded, "Yes. I'm just surprised at how much everyone seems to care about Ben. I've never seen anything like it. It's a lot to take in."

"Of course we do. He's a great kid, Simon"—Ms. Thorne paused, as if deciding what to say next—"I know it's our job to help him, and so it might seem like that's all it is. A job. It's not though; for us it's more than that. Ben's special, and you've all been through so much. It means a lot to us to see him succeed. It means a lot to see your family succeed. It's something we hold near and dear to our hearts because to us, you're like family."

"Thank you," Simon told her, startled at the kindness of what she'd just said. "Thank you so much."

Standing up, he nodded a quick goodbye, walking quickly through the school and out the double doors to his car. He made it almost all the way home before he started sobbing. For the first time in a long time, his tears weren't filled with sadness; they were filled with gratitude.

10

"I FEEL DIFFERENT," OLIVE OBSERVED.

Michael sparkled. "How?" he asked.

Olive thought for a moment, pondering how to best describe her feelings. "When I first got here, all I cared about was my family. I wanted to go back to them so badly, I would have done anything to get back to them. It hurt so much to think of what my leaving did to them. It still hurts, and if I had the chance, I'd go back in a heartbeat, but those feelings aren't as strong anymore. They don't consume me as they once did. Now I feel...almost pulled in a different direction, somehow away from them, and I'm okay with that. I never thought I'd say that"—Olive laughed—"I still love them more than ever, but I have this overwhelming belief that they're going to be okay."

Michael smiled.

"You already knew all of this, didn't you?" Olive questioned lightly.

"Sometimes saying it out loud makes it more real," Michael replied.

Olive smiled at the simple truth of his words. He was always filled with surprises in the ways he helped her heal and move on to what she was meant to be. He was always gently guiding her to become more than she was. Sometimes it was a little uncomfortable, and sometimes it just plain hurt, but she knew whatever she was going to go through would help her learn and grow. She knew he'd always be by her side and that she could always trust in him.

Olive felt a nudge and looked up. "I think I'm almost ready," she replied to Michael, "but first, before I let them go, I'd like to do one last thing."

Michael smiled, shimmered, gave her peace. He knew even though she was ready it was going to be hard for her.

"Will you take me?" she asked quietly, "To say goodbye?"

"I will if you need me to," Michael replied, "But why don't you try it by yourself this time."

"Please come with me?" Olive pleaded, a flicker of fear came and went, peace quickly filling its place.

Michael sparkled as Olive grabbed his hand and pulled him through.

* * *

They were standing beside Beckett's bed, and Olive could feel her heart breaking. She loved him so much, how could she leave him again? It wasn't fair. She watched as his chest rose and fell with each breath, and noticed how he had grown in the months she'd been gone. She wished she could hug him. Hold him tighter than she'd ever held him before. But she couldn't, and she started to cry.

She felt Michael's hand on her shoulder and leaned into his peace.

He explained, "It's not really goodbye, Olive. It's just letting go." Michael paused, then asked "Do you remember how to connect?"

Olive nodded and closed her eyes. She could feel Beckett all around her. She remembered the last time she'd done this that Michael had given her light, to help connect. She wondered if he had forgotten this time and just as soon as that thought entered her mind, she heard Michael's silent words, *You can do this on your own, Olive. You don't need me anymore.*

His voice was like a whisper, but she knew he hadn't used his voice; he was talking to her in his mind. It was something he'd been doing more often lately. Realizing that she *didn't* need him anymore, she worried he might leave her, but she felt his presence strongly behind her and heard him communicate, *Focus, Olive.*

She took a deep breath in and thought of Beckett. She remembered his bright smile that was a perfect match to hers, his laugh that could make anyone else in earshot crack up, and the way he loved with a fierceness that always took Olive by surprise. *He's so beautiful,* she thought and heard Michael agree, *He's perfect.*

Slowly, slowly, she felt his spirit surrounding hers and gently connecting with him.

* * *

Beckett was sitting in the booth they always sat in when they went to get ice cream. He was about to take his first lick off his ice cream cone when he heard the door open. He knew all at once that his mom was there too.

"Mom!" he cried as she appeared in front of him, "You're so sparkly! Just like the angel that was here before." He laughed and jumped up to hug her.

She hugged him tight, as tight as she could, and didn't let go until he laughed again, telling her she was holding on too tight.

"Sorry, buddy," replied Olive and then laughed along with him. "I've just missed you so much, and I've missed hugging you too." She breathed him in as she kissed the top of his head. "How have things been going?" she inquired, sitting down beside him.

Beckett considered her as he licked his cone. "Seriously, Mom, you're super sparkly," he remarked, studying her some more and then adding, "I like it!" Taking another lick of his cone, he went on, "I'm not afraid anymore, Mom. You know, of Dad leaving. Your friend helped me feel better, and I do."

"Good, I'm glad you feel better. How's school?" Olive asked. She wished she could sit here with him forever, soaking it in.

Beckett frowned, explaining, "It's okay. I'm not supposed to talk about the angel there because some kids don't believe me. But it's okay because I know it was real. I was mad about it for a while, but I'm okay with it now. Plus, I can talk about it as much as I want at home with Ben and Dad and Gizzy."

Olive smiled, saying, "I'm glad you are talking with them. It's good to talk about how we feel, right? What else do you want to tell me?" Feeling Michael, she knew it was almost time to go.

Beckett nodded and asked, "Did your angel tell you something? I just heard him, but I don't know what he said." He looked around to see if he could spot him. When he couldn't, he shrugged his shoulders and took another lick of his cone.

Surprised, Olive explained, "He just told me it's almost time for me to go. I'm kind of surprised you heard him!"

"Oh, I hear him all the time. You know, if I'm scared or sad, he helps me feel better. He visits me a lot to make sure I'm okay"—Beckett paused—"I don't want you to go yet, Mom."

Again, Olive was surprised. "I had no idea Michael was visiting you," she said and then thought for a second, adding, "That makes me really happy." She paused to look at Beckett, taking everything in for one last time. "I love you Beckett. So much. You know that right?"

Beckett nodded and started to cry, begging, "Please don't go, Mom."

Olive felt Michael give her peace. She asked for the perfect words to explain to Beckett what was going to happen next, and she felt them come. She leaned over and gave Beckett one last hug. When she finally let go, she sat back against the booth and tried to smile. "I know you don't want me to leave Beckett, but I have to, for a while."

Beckett started to cry harder, and Olive pulled him into her arms, telling him, "It's hard to understand, I know. But I promise you, I will always be here if you need me, okay? All you need to do is think of me or call out to me, and I'll be there." Olive wasn't sure how she knew this was true, but she did. She knew deep down that if her family needed her, she'd be able to be there in a flash.

There wasn't anything holding her back from her family or keeping her away. She knew she needed to finally let them go completely, so they could heal and so she could move forward toward her purpose. They all needed to look towards what came next, and part of that was letting go and moving on.

Beckett wiped his eyes and looked up at her to inquire, "How will I know you are here?"

Olive was about to say what everyone says—that he'd feel her in his heart. She believed that to be true, but she wanted to give him a more concrete sign, something that would show him without a doubt that she was right where she promised she'd be. She thought for a minute and then had an idea. She promised, "I'll give you a sign that I'm there, so you know."

He smiled and asked, "What kind of sign?"

"I'll do this," Olive explained, taking a deep breath and blowing the napkins, so they fluttered around and off the table. Beckett laughed, and Olive felt her heart shine. "I'll make something move, and I'll try to make you laugh, and then you'll know. Okay?"

"Every time I call?" Beckett questioned, solemnly.

"Every time," Olive promised, and she knew it was true.

Beckett giggled and pointed at Olive, remarking, "Look at your heart, it's so bright! You're so pretty, Mom. I love you."

Olive smiled back at Beckett and took his small hands in hers, explaining, "It's time for me to go."

Beckett's smile slowly melted away, and he became serious. "Okay," he said softly.

"I want to tell you something before I leave," she stated, watching Beckett as he nodded. "I want you to remember these things whenever you're sad or you miss me or if you're mad at Dad or Ben or just having a hard time, okay?"

He nodded again, and she could tell he was trying with all of his might to be brave for her.

"I love you so much, and I'm so sorry I left you. I am so lucky to be your mom, and I want you to always remember how amazing you are and how proud of you I am. I love the way your heart shines, Beckett. It shines brighter than mine. I wish you could see it."

She smiled down at him, and he lifted his hands and brushed away the tears she hadn't even known were falling.

"It's true," she said as she placed her hand over his heart. She felt it beating and could feel the love and kindness that was held inside. "I know sometimes you think you need to make everyone else happy, and that's such a good thing. But I want you to remember that sometimes all you can do for someone is just love them. Just love them and know it's not always up to you to make sure they are okay. Sometimes they just need to find their own way, and it's okay for you to let them do that." Olive paused, caught her breath, and continued, "But the one thing I want you to remember the most is simply this—I love you. I love you with every part of me, and I will never stop loving you, no matter what. No matter what."

"I love you too, Mommy," Beckett stated, his bottom lip starting to shake.

"It's important that you know it's okay to let me go now, okay? It's important for you to do that," Olive said, slowly pulling away.

"No, Mommy!" Beckett screamed, "I can't!" He sobbed.

"Beckett," Olive stated in her best mom voice, "It's okay. I need to let you go too. It's hard, I know it's so hard, but this is what we need to do now. Remember, I'll always be here for you"—she took his head in her hands and wiped away his tears—"Let's do it together, okay? We'll count to three, and we'll do it together."

"You promise you'll be here if I need you?" asked Beckett with a hiccup.

"I promise," Olive answered, holding tight to Beckett's hands once more. "Ready?" she asked, shakily.

"No, Mommy," Beckett said sadly, "I don't want to."

Looking into his eyes, she said encouragingly, "I don't want to do this either, Beckett. But Michael showed me how important it is. Letting go will help us all to move on and get better. Will you do it with me? Can we be brave together and let go?"

"Okay," Beckett agreed reluctantly.

His eyes were full of sadness, and it crushed her to know she was hurting him once again.

Show him how you feel. Show him how you know it's okay. She felt Michael's words like a soft whisper against her cheek. She knew what to do without even having to ask and recognized in that moment how much Michael had taught her.

Focusing her attention on Beckett, she pulled forth her feelings of peace, happiness, love, and joy, and gave them to him. She saw them move like a golden light from her hands into his. She saw surprise and contentment fill Beckett's face and was surprised herself when she felt love and understanding flow back into her through him.

"I'm ready," she heard Beckett say strongly and felt that it was true.

Olive took a deep breath; she let it out. "One," she said, looking into his eyes for the last time. "Two," she continued, squeezing his hands tight, for the last time. "Three," she said, voice cracking.

Pausing, they looked into each other's eyes and a million memories flashed between them, as together they said the last four words either of them wanted to say, "I let you go."

For a moment there was absolute silence, and the single thought ringing through Olive's mind was *What have I done?* Then she felt Michael's hand on her shoulder, and she spun around to face him, tears filling her eyes.

"I know that was hard, but I'm proud of you. You did a great job of transferring your feelings to Beckett. Those feelings are what helped him understand and let go," conveyed Michael. He smiled at her and filled her with his love.

The feeling was still big and powerful, but she no longer had to close her eyes to take it in. She could feel all of what he was giving her and not have to take it so slowly anymore. She thought of Beckett, remembering how he had given her love back. "How could he do that?" she questioned Michael, "Send his feelings back to me? I thought it was only something *we* could do."

Michael shimmered so brightly that this time she did have to close her eyes.

"I've told you before that when you are on Earth, you forget some of the things you knew how to do before you got there. Some people haven't forgotten as much. Beckett is one of those few people."

"How?" Olive asked, stunned.

Michael shined happily, explaining, "It's part of his path on Earth, to be able to communicate in a way that other people can connect to easily. People with this gift have a way of giving and showing love that can come across a little strongly, but it's a key part in connecting with others emotionally, so they can feel his deep understanding and love for them."

Olive laughed as Michael showed her what he knew of Beckett's path. "That makes so much sense! I always said he loved in the fiercest way I'd ever seen before," she remarked.

Michael laughed too, and Olive was reminded of the wind chime that hung on their front porch. She wondered if her laugh sounded like a wind chime or something else.

"Bells," Michael told her, and when he saw she didn't quite understand, he added, "Your laugh, it sounds more like bells than a wind chime."

I'm still getting used to that, she thought.

Michael sparkled a little, silently communicating, *It's time.*

Ben, thought Olive.

With a heavy heart she glanced over her shoulder at Beckett, sending him love and sparkly blessings, as they left.

* * *

As Olive stood at the foot of the bed and looked down at Ben, her heart shattered. How could she let this boy go too? How could she look into his eyes and tell him she was leaving. Again? She saw how he had grown too and felt a deep sorrow thinking of all the things she'd miss out on. The not so great band concerts and the almost too close to call baseball games. The days that were filled with excitement, the days where the only thing the boys could find to do was pick on each other, and every day in between. She'd miss every single moment, and when her family looked back on those times, all she would be was an afterthought.

Even now, knowing what she knew to be true, she still would give anything to go back to them. She felt Michael beside her and turned her attention to why she was here in the first place.

Olive took a deep breath to quiet her heart and closed her eyes, waiting to feel Ben's spirit. His spirit was more gentle than Beckett's, and it took a little bit longer to sense him. Remembering to be gentle, Olive pulled herself back a little when she finally felt him and then slowly, slowly made contact.

* * *

Ben was sitting in their backyard on the porch swing, deep in thought as he looked out past the edge of the grass and into the forest beyond. Olive had loved that porch swing. She remembered how she had begged and begged Simon to put one up after they had finished their patio. There had been a million and one reasons why he hadn't wanted a porch swing, so Olive had been surprised when she had come home one evening after a PTC meeting at school to find the three of them swinging in it, big grins on their faces.

She had stopped in her tracks, frozen with disbelief, until Ben had called out to her, "Come on, Mom! Try it out!" From that moment on, whenever she'd had a free minute or just needed to think, she would head out to the porch swing. Beckett had put it perfectly when he'd observed, "Everyone has a special place in our house. Mine is the big, squishy chair. Dad and Ben's is the couch, and the porch swing is Mom's."

As Ben swung back and forth slowly, he thought of his mom and knew deep down she was there with him. He turned his head towards the house and saw her. "Mom," he whispered, thinking it was too good to be true. He still missed her so much, and though he tried as hard as he could to be brave, there were days when he wasn't sure he could make it without crying.

"Ben," Olive said simply, as she sat down beside him and pulled him into a hug. She could tell he was struggling not to cry, and so she held him tighter. "It's okay," she told him quietly, "It's okay to cry."

Ben felt his mom let go a little as she rubbed her hand up and down his back, and he started to sob. He missed this, his mom holding him, rubbing his back. He wished he had let her do it more often when s

He wasn't sure how he knew, but he knew she was here

he leaned into his mom's embrace, soaking in every last pi

"I've missed you," she stated as she kissed the top of h

moment to breath in his sweet scent. "I hear you've been doing awesome in school." She smiled at his shocked look.

"How do you know?" he asked, incredulous.

"I'm your mom, I know everything," she joked, then squeezed him tight and added, "I can see you sometimes, from where I am, and I was there at the meeting with Dad at school"—Olive laughed—"He was nervous. Did you know that?"

Ben nodded and smiled a little, thinking of his dad the day of the meeting.

"He talked to me before he went inside. He asked me to give him a sign, so he would know he was doing the right thing." Olive leaned back against the swing, thinking of Simon.

"So did you?" Ben asked, intrigued.

"I did," Olive replied, smiling down at Ben, "He said one sign could be sneezing consecutively three times, like I used to do."

Ben laughed, inquiring, "You made Dad sneeze?"

Olive laughed too and explained, "No. He was too nervous. It wouldn't have worked. But Ms. Thorne wasn't too nervous, and so I made *her* sneeze three times. Plus, she knows what we've been working towards, so I thought that could be a good sign for Dad to take her advice, if he needed any."

Ben smiled, then asked, "Why does it matter if someone is nervous?"

Olive thought for a while, considering how to best explain. "I guess the easiest way to say it is that you can't get through to someone who is nervous. Or someone who is busy thinking a million other things. That's why it's easier for me to visit you when you are asleep. You are more open and receptive to it."

Ben nodded, looking up at Olive. Then he asked, "Are you here to say goodbye?" His eyes glistened.

"I am," Olive replied softly.

Ben clenched his jaw, and Olive saw herself in him. There were many parts of Ben that he had inherited from Olive, from his dimples and the shape of his eyes, to the need to always be strong for his family, no matter what.

Her heart broke for him when she saw all that he would need to perience to get through this, but she lightened a little when she saw how far he had already come. He was determined, a hard worker, and Olive took comfort in the fact that those qualities would help him along the way.

"It's not going to be easy," Olive told him, looking into eyes that mirrored hers, "but you will get through this, and I think you will make something beautiful out of your pain. I'm not sure what," she added when he looked at her confused, "but I know your going through this isn't for nothing."

"I don't understand what you mean," he replied sadly, and Olive realized she had revealed too much in her need to comfort him.

"I know you don't. I'm sorry, Ben. One day you will understand, and then you can remember this moment." She hugged him close to her, as tightly as she could, knowing this was her last chance. "I'm so proud of you, Ben."

"Please don't go, Mommy," he pleaded, and Olive, realizing he hadn't called her mommy in years, started to cry. "Please don't cry," he said and reached up to wipe away her tears.

Olive let her tears flow because they felt good and because after her good-byes, she would leave her body form behind for good, so she wanted to feel this moment. Really feel this moment. "Ben," she sniffed, "My Ben. I love you so much. You made me a mom"—she smiled down at him—"You showed me how to love with every part of me. Before you, I never knew a person could love that much. I never knew that kind of love existed until you. You were the one who taught me what it was like to believe in myself. To really, truly believe in who I was. You even helped me love myself."

"I did?" Ben questioned.

Olive nodded and took a moment to compose herself as Ben leaned his head on her shoulder. She leaned her head against his and explained, "You did. You looked at me with eyes that matched my own, and they were so full of trust and belief and acceptance and love, all for me! I started looking at myself in a different light from that moment on. I was able to let the things I didn't like about myself go a little bit easier because you had shown me, in your own way, how beautiful I was."

"Wow," Ben said, and Olive saw his heart light up, big and bright. It lit hers up, too.

"Mom, you're so sparkly," Ben observed with a laugh as he touched Olive's face.

Olive felt Michael, and she knew it was time. "Ben," she said, her voice shaking, "I want to tell you some things, and I want you to remember them. Don't forget, okay?"

Ben nodded. He started crying silently.

Why does this have to be so hard? Olive thought, and she heard Michael, *I'm so proud of how strong you are, Olive.*

To Ben she said, "We need to say goodbye to each other now. We need to let each other go." She took a breath before she went on and felt Michael give her strength. "Do you remember Michael, my angel?" she asked.

Ben nodded and looked towards the direction Olive had come from.

Olive glanced over her shoulder and saw Michael. She turned back to Ben to explain, "I told him I didn't want to say goodbye. I said it would be too hard"—Ben was crying harder now, and so was Olive—"But he told me we needed to do this, Ben. For us to move on and get better, we need to let go of each other."

"No, Mom!" Ben cried, and he hugged Olive even tighter to him.

If Olive thought her heart had broken before now, she was wrong. That was nothing, nothing compared to the piercing pain she was experiencing at this moment.

"Shh," Olive coaxed, rubbing his back, "I want to tell you something now, so pay attention. I love you so much, Ben. There will never, ever be a day that goes by that I don't love you. I promise that things will get easier, but you need to let them. You need to know that it's okay to be happy, and to laugh and have fun, even without me, okay? I want you to do that for me. I want you to do what makes you happy because that will make me happy. My one wish that I have had since the day you and Beckett were born was that you'd both be happy. That's it."

Olive sat back and looked Ben in the eyes, then continued, "It's that simple, Ben. I swear it, that's all I've ever wanted for you. All I've ever done was to ensure that you'd be happy. I'm sure I messed up a bunch of times or made you mad, especially when I took away electronics. But"—Olive paused and smiled at Ben when he cracked a smile—"I was doing my best."

"It's just so hard without you. How can you know it'll get better?" Ben asked hoarsely.

Show him, she heard Michael whisper, so she took Ben's hands in hers and closed her eyes. She took what she knew, and she gave it to Ben. She showed him how he would heal, how Simon and Beckett and her mom would heal. She gave him peace and love and understanding, and let it flow towards him without holding back. For a second she thought it might be too much, but she saw how he took it in stride. How he was overcome with relief and comfort and a peace that had been missing as long as she had. She saw him sparkle and glow and how his heart was healing in time with hers.

She heard him think, *I'm ready,* and knew that it was true. She opened her eyes and saw him smiling back at her.

"You really are telling the truth," he stated with such certainty and light that Olive laughed.

"I am," confirmed Olive, remembering one more thing she had wanted to say, "I told Beckett that if ever he needs me, all he needs to do is think of me or call for me. The same goes for you too."

Ben nodded, swallowed, and asked what she knew he'd ask, "How will I know you are here? I hope you don't tell me that I can feel you inside because even though that is probably true, I would rather sneeze three times like Ms. Thorne."

Olive laughed. "How about I do this?" she suggested and blew the leaves that had fallen off a nearby tree and onto the porch swing, sending them twirling through the air.

Ben laughed, questioning, "But what if there aren't any leaves?"

"Then I'll make something else move," Olive replied, swinging them back and forth on the porch swing.

"You promise? That you'll be here when I need you?" Ben asked, just to be sure.

"I promise." Olive gave him one more tight, tight squeeze then asked, "You ready?"

"No," he answered, voice cracking.

"Me neither," Olive confessed, "But we need to do this for each other. So let's do it together."

"I love you, Mom, so much," Ben told her.

"I love you too, Ben, so much," she said, and he smiled up at her, dimples flashing.

She would miss him so much, too much. It hurt to think about, so she did what she knew she needed to do. She grabbed his hands. "One," she said, squeezing his hands for the last time. "Two," she said, looking into his eyes for the last time. Memories passed between them in the seconds that followed, and it took all her strength, but she finally said, "Three," her voice cracking.

Though she knew he would be okay, the last four words she needed to say broke her. "I let you go," they said in unison as Ben disappeared in front of her eyes, and there was nothing left for her to do but wonder if she'd made a mistake.

"I know this is hard," Michael told her, touching her shoulder as she cried, "but it will get easier."

"I know," Olive agreed. Drying her eyes, she looked down at Ben as he lay sleeping. He looked so peaceful lying there. Olive took one last look, memorizing every last detail.

She remembered when he was little and how he wanted her to lie with him until he fell asleep. She had eventually convinced him to let her sit on the floor by his bed, each night inching closer and closer towards the doorway and her freedom beyond. There were nights she had been so frustrated that she couldn't just say goodnight and walk away, so desperate for her alone time she would often lose her patience. She could remember those feelings so clearly, but looking back, she wished she had enjoyed that time with him. He was getting older each day, and he wasn't going to need her forever.

She felt Michael beside her and knew it was time to go. Olive leaned over and kissed Ben on the cheek. When she gave him peace, sent him love, he smiled a little in his sleep, and she was reminded, once again, that he would be okay.

* * *

They were in her and Simon's bedroom. Olive was confused, and when she turned to Michael, he nodded towards the bed, where Olive saw Simon. He was stretched out haphazardly across the bed, snoring quietly.

Olive noticed the pile of laundry half folded next to the bed and how Simon badly needed a haircut. She saw that her hand cream and the book she'd been reading before she died were still on the nightstand. She looked in the closet and noticed her clothes still hanging on their hangers, the pajamas she'd worn the night before she'd left, still in a bunch in the corner of the closet.

Traces of her were still everywhere, and though she was happy he hadn't erased her every presence, she knew this wasn't good if they were going to move on. Her heart broke in the way it breaks when you feel like there is nothing you can do to help someone you love who is hurting. When you can see exactly what it is they need to do to heal but know that they have to do it for themselves in order for it to happen.

"Oh Simon," Olive said quietly, and at the sound of her voice, Simon stirred in his sleep. "What can I do to help him?"

"Do what you did with Ben and Beckett," Michael suggested.

"But how? I haven't been able to connect with him before," Olive whispered.

"It's going to be different with him. You won't meet him in a dream like you did with your boys. When you feel his spirit, show him what you want him to know with your thoughts. He's not as open as your boys are, so you won't have as much time," Michael shimmered.

"Will he remember?" Olive asked.

Michael sparkled, answering, "Yes. What you show him will be very clear, and when he wakes up, he might be confused by what happened, but it will help him a great deal because it will have a profound effect on him. He will know you were here, but his rational mind will have a hard time making sense of it. He will think back to what you show him many times, and it will bring him comfort, so use this time wisely."

Olive was afraid. What if she didn't have enough time to show Simon all of what she wanted him to know? What if she was too fast or too strong or took too much time? She felt Michael give her peace and knew that what she gave to Simon would be just what he needed. *Thank you*, she thought and Michael grew bright.

He brightened and brightened, until Olive looked over at him in alarm. "What are you doing?" she asked, worried Simon would wake up and she wouldn't be able to connect.

"Adults are more difficult to connect with because they are usually more closed off. I'm helping to raise his vibration a little, so it is easier for you to find him," Michael explained softly, "It's time, go now."

Olive closed her eyes and took a deep breath in. When she let it out, she was slammed with Michael's energy. He pulled her in with him, and when she felt what she knew was Simon, he drew back.

Connecting with Simon was different than connecting with Ben or Beckett. Simon's energy was tighter, more compact, so Olive had to work at finding a way in to match up with him. She thought of what she loved about Simon—how he was such a great father that it took her by surprise sometimes, how he was kind and compassionate towards people he didn't even know, always willing to lend a hand, how he could fix anything, no matter how difficult, how he always knew the best way to make Olive laugh when she was down.

She saw Simon's face flash before her eyes and knew they were connected. She felt him jump back, startled and unsure, then relax when he realized she was there with him.

Don't be afraid, she said, *I just came to say goodbye*. Gently, she showed him what she wanted him to know, what she hoped he would remember. That she loved him and that she was okay. That she had visited the boys. That she missed them with a longing she couldn't put into words. That she was proud of him and knew he would be okay without her. She showed him Ms. Thorne's three sneezes to acknowledge that she'd been there with him. She showed him why they needed to let each other go, that it was okay to move on. She showed him that she believed in him, and even though she knew she needed to be careful, she took everything she had and put it together to show him how much she loved him. *I LOVE YOU!!!* she screamed with all of her energy, sending sparkling rain showers down onto Simon as he was sleeping. She surprised herself as she showed him that it was okay if he found love again, but she knew it was true and she meant it. She showed him how much she wanted him and the boys to be happy. *I love you*, she said again, more gently this time. And as Simon faded away, she sent him love and peace and hope for a better tomorrow, her wishes falling like tears from her heart as she finally, finally let him go.

* * *

Simon woke the next morning with a lightness in his heart he hadn't felt in a long time. He sat up slowly, stretching, listening for any sounds of the boys.

Hearing nothing, he relaxed back against the soft headboard. Then he remembered.

His heart swelled in his chest, and tears came to his eyes when he realized it hadn't been just a dream. Olive had actually been there with him, leaving him with a heartbreakingly beautiful message and then saying goodbye. Rationally, it seemed crazy and unlikely. The hopes of a desperate man who each day was coming closer and closer to giving up, but he knew, he just *knew*, it had been real.

He still missed her so much, but he had a new sense of hope filling his heart. Hope that he could move on, that *they* could move on, without her. Never forgetting, always remembering, but healing and living a life she would have wanted them to live.

The belief that this might be possible for him had never been this close before, and he grabbed hold of it, determined to never let it go, no matter what. Simon knew the next couple of months were going to be difficult for them. Summer break was fast approaching, as well as both Beckett's and Ben's birthdays.

Olive had absolutely loved summer break. Summer was her favorite time of year, and being able to spend it with her boys was what she had looked forward to all year long. She had an ongoing list she kept tucked in her purse of what she wanted to do the coming summer. Simon sometimes joked with her, telling her they wouldn't get much of a 'break' if she thought they were going to complete the whole list in three short months.

"We're not going to do *everything*, but it's good to have options," she told him once, and Simon knew the list gave Olive something to dream about when the days got shorter and the air got colder. Olive made the summers special for the boys, and he hoped he could somehow do the same. He wasn't sure just how they were going to get through those special days ahead without her, but he knew, deep down, that they would.

His hope that they might not only manage, but maybe even succeed without Olive, was changing into something strong and true and real. Thanks to Olive, he had a crystal-clear picture of what that would be like and how he could make it happen. Would it be challenging? Yes, but Simon could feel himself growing stronger with each breath he took. Feeling like he didn't have a minute to lose, he jumped up and headed into the shower, thanking Olive for giving him what he had needed the most. A new outlook on life.

By the time Simon got showered, dressed, and ready for work, the boys were already downstairs. He noticed they were eating birthday cake-flavored Pop-Tarts and drinking Sprite. Mara had been back at her place for about a week, and Simon hadn't quite gotten the hot breakfast thing down just yet. Their goodbyes had been tearful and hard on the boys, but Mara had promised to come and visit soon. They all knew she would. Mara was nothing if not good to her word.

Simon decided to let it go (again, yesterday was candy corn and hot chocolate), promising himself he'd do better. He hoped their teachers would forgive him. Maybe he could have the boys run around the outside of the house a few times before school? He wondered how much energy that would burn. He wondered if running around like crazy people would just get them more worked up. He wondered what the neighbors would think.

"Dad!" Beckett screeched, jumping up and grabbing onto Simon's back, pulling him away from his thoughts.

"Whoah, bud. Watch those hands! I don't want to have Pop-Tarts all over my shirt, people might think I'm weird," Simon joked as Beckett slid down to the floor and hopped back to his chair, taking a big gulp of Sprite.

"Too late, you already are weird, Dad," Ben replied, trying to keep a straight face. No longer being able to hold it, he stuffed a Pop-Tart into his mouth and leaned back in his chair.

"Ha-ha," Simon countered, turning on the coffee pot and longing for Mara's coffee.

"It's LOL, Dad, duh," Beckett giggled.

"Well, you two are sure in a good mood," Simon observed, grabbing his favorite mug out of the cupboard and ruffling Beckett's hair as he walked past.

"You are too, Dad," Ben stated, a small smile playing hopefully on his face.

Simon poured himself some coffee, filling it to the brim, and went to sit at the table across from the boys. "I am, and I have good reason to be"—he took a sip of his coffee, then continued, excited to share his news—"Mom visited me last night."

"WHAT!" Ben and Beckett cried at the same time, eyes wide.

"She visited us too," Ben confided. "We were just talking about it before you came down."

Simon should have been surprised, but he wasn't. He had been becoming more of a believer in what he considered to be spiritual things unseen by the rest of us. If he had any doubt left in his mind, last night put that to rest. As unexpected as it was for him to admit his belief in things unseen (he would have called himself crazy only last year), it was a comfort to know Olive was, in her own way, watching out for them. Knowing wherever she was, she wasn't suffering, but okay, happy even, gave him peace.

Leaning in towards Ben and Beckett, Simon smiled. "Tell me," he said, "what happened." And they spent the rest of the morning before school and work, huddled around the table, the sounds of joy and happiness filling their home.

They wouldn't have seen it, would have almost missed it, if Simon hadn't noticed and called the boys into the kitchen, instructing them to grab their homework off the island. Just as Ben and Beckett rounded the corner of the mudroom and stepped into the kitchen, their papers blew off the island and floated toward them, landing at their feet.

Beckett and Ben looked at each other and laughed, as Simon, confused, stared dumbfounded at the island, wondering where the breeze had come from. Simon felt her blow by him and ruffle his too long hair, give him a soft kiss on the cheek, and then she was gone.

"Bye, Mom!" the boys said in unison, as they grabbed their backpacks and made their way to the car, someone shouting, "Coming, Dad?"

A few minutes passed, and Ben stuck his head into the kitchen, wondering what was keeping his father. "Dad!" he called loudly, snapping Simon out of his trance.

Simon turned and looked at Ben, declaring, "Wow." A smile slowly spread across his face.

Ben smiled a little. "Come on, Dad," he urged as he grabbed Simon's hand and pulled him out of the house.

Simon stumbled out the door and into the car, amazed at what had just happened. "Wow," he said again, starting the car and backing out of the garage.

"You'll get used to it, Dad," Beckett declared and laughed as Ben rolled his eyes, pretending to be embarrassed.

"That was awesome!" Simon exclaimed, laughing to himself.

"Okay, Dad, we get it!" Ben teased, elbowing Beckett in the ribs.

The few-minute drive to school was spent in a peaceful, reflective silence. "Have a good day, boys," Simon said, gently slapping them on their shoulders as they got out of the car.

Simon watched as they walked into school together, laughing and talking animatedly. They were lucky to have each other, and he was lucky to have them.

As Simon pulled onto the highway, making his way to work, he smiled at how good he felt. How *great* he felt! He knew things wouldn't be easy, that there were hard days to come, but he felt good right now, in this moment, and this moment was what mattered. He gave himself a mental high-five, thinking about how great the day was turning out to be.

But then he turned on the radio and heard Ed Sheeran's song "Supermarket Flowers" and started to cry. He never used to be this sensitive, crying over songs on the radio or cheesy commercials on TV. He wondered if there would ever be a time where he would recognize his old self, but he could barely remember who that was anymore. Did he want to go back to the man he was before? He wasn't sure. There was something inside of him that made him feel like the person he was growing into was the person he was always meant to become. Maybe things would never go back to what they used to be. *But maybe*, he thought, *that was okay.*

11

SHE COULD FEEL HIM AGAIN. SHE CLOSED HER EYES AS SHE TURNED around to face Him. She was surprised by the ease of how she could slip in and out of form, knowing the reason she went into form was because it was a comfort for her. She wondered if it would always be this way or if there would be a time when she would no longer need her body to feel safe.

She could feel Him chuckling gently, it was like a soft buzz that made her want to sneeze, but it felt good.

"Hello, Olive," He said, then added silently, *You won't always need your body. As time goes on, it'll disappear and you won't even notice.*

Olive smiled and dipped her head to her chest. He was still big and hard to take in, but she was slowly getting used to the way He felt, and she knew, instinctively, once she no longer needed her body that it would be easier to see Him.

"I'm so proud of you," He told her, "Look at all you've done. Your family is starting to heal, and so are you."

She felt His love surrounding her, and tears came to her eyes because she wasn't used to feeling something so all-encompassing and beautiful. His love was so pure and unconditional, so full of acceptance and kindness, she had to laugh at herself for being so surprised at it; of course it would be like this—He was love.

We all are, he whispered to her, at the same time as the thought entered her mind, and they laughed together because she just realized again how connected everyone was.

"Are you ready to see the plan?" He asked, and when she could only nod, He showed it to her.

Tears filled her eyes as she saw how beautiful and perfect it was, and even though having to leave her family still hurt more than she could put into words, she saw now how everything fit into place. She saw how important it was and how she could do great things. She saw how this had been part of her plan all along and realized with a start and a small laugh that she had known about it long before she was born.

How can this be? she wondered, and at the same time, knowing flowed over her like a waterfall, and she understood it all completely.

She started to cry because it was all too much to take in, the sudden clarity made her lose her breath, and she started to fall to the ground. He caught her before she fell all the way, and holding her gently, He gave her peace.

"I've got you," He promised, "I will always have you. Always."

Olive squeezed her eyes shut tight. Everything she was feeling, it was all too much, and she didn't know how she could make it through all the overwhelming feelings and into acceptance. Then she realized that if she let her body go, the feelings might not be as intense, and it might be easier.

So she did. She let it go, let it slide away, and the overpowering sensations slowly dissolved into something bright and pulsing. A steady beat that was now comforting, and she understood in that moment that what she had let go hadn't really been her body. It had been her fear.

With this realization came the awareness that she could see Him now, she could take Him all in without having to turn away or hold back. She felt as light and bright and free as she had ever felt before, and she started to laugh because of Him, and it was beautiful.

He was bright and big and boundless. He was everywhere, in everything and everybody. He was sparkling in the ocean and glittering in the sky. He was shimmering in the hearts of each and every person in the entire world, and Olive knew He was shining inside of her.

You are all a part of me, He confirmed, *and I a part of you.*

What Olive felt at that moment was so big, and all that she could now see made her heart feel so happy that it felt like it might explode. For a minute she thought it had exploded because when she looked down all she saw was bright, bright sparkling light, shooting out from all around her. Then Michael was beside her laughing, and she realized that it wasn't her heart that was exploding. It was her. And she wasn't exploding, she was transforming. She was becoming something more than she'd ever been, and she knew in that instant that Michael had been sent to do more than just help her heal. He had been sent to show her how to become an angel.

When it was over, and she was ready, she turned to Michael. It had taken a while. Not the becoming, that had been the easy part, but the accepting. It had felt weird to think of herself as an angel, but Olive felt sure this was where she was supposed to be. There was no doubt in her mind. She knew it was right and so she was happy.

"Welcome home," he stated simply.

Olive laughed as she looked down at herself, shimmering almost brighter than Michael.

He smiled at her and she could tell he was proud.

"There's someone," he said, "that I think you should meet."

Olive followed as Michael led the way.

* * *

Simon had been completely out of his league when trying to decide what to do with the boys during their time off of school. When Olive had been alive, she had stayed home with them and he hadn't had to think about a thing, barring the occasional lunch date they sometimes set up.

The boys had always loved to visit Simon at work but weren't always the quietest visitors, so Simon usually chose a day when he knew more of his associates would be out of the office, so the noise wouldn't matter as much.

Now though, setting up the summer plans had been completely up to him, and he had no idea where to start. Cue Ms. Thorne, who had given him a plethora of ideas. So much so that he had been overwhelmed with the many choices.

With the help of Ms. Thorne, he narrowed it down to three choices, and from there let the boys decide. There was summer day camp at the YMCA. Something else called Funtastic Summer was being offered through the local community ed. Option three was the school's summer program, Diary of an Awesome Summer, which was supposed to be *Diary of a Wimpy Kid*-inspired, though he really wasn't sure what that meant. "What does that even mean?" he asked the boys, and Ben just rolled his eyes in response.

The eye roll had become a typical response from Ben. Simon knew most parents would hate it, but he took it as a good thing. It made him feel like they were getting back to normal.

"I don't know about you guys, but Funtastic Summer sounds cool!" Simon commented with forced enthusiasm. He still wasn't sure what they thought about their new summer schedule. He knew the adjustment from summers at home with Mom to going to a summer program four days of the week could be difficult. They had handouts for each choice spread out on the table, and they were gathered around, looking each one over closely.

"Really, Dad? Really?" Beckett replied sarcastically, filling Simon with joy.

He knew his kids sometimes thought he was a little bit of a 'weirdo,' but he didn't care. The mocking tone of Beckett's voice made Simon want to grab him and hold him close, spinning around in circles like he used to do when they were little. But Simon knew better, so he forced himself to stay put and act like it was all no big deal. It was though, to him it was.

He could see them getting there, reaching out to their new normal, trying it out for themselves. So far it felt good, as good as it could, considering. He felt hope light up inside of him, and he smiled at his boys. They were growing up and he was so proud of them. "Yeah, but look here," he said, pointing to the description, "It says you get to roller-skate with cartoon characters and swim with funky fish! You also get to create origami animals, even make your own zoo!"

Beckett took a closer look at the description and made a thoughtful face, wondering if making origami would be worth suffering through having to go roller-skating.

"I wonder where they get the funky fish?" Simon pondered, "You don't think they bring in a bunch of tropical fish, do you? That would be cool, but then how would that work? You'd need a ton of salt water for that … and where would they put it?" Simon thought about the logistics as Ben and Beckett gave each other a knowing look.

"Naw, Dad. Those fish are all plastic anyways. They just load 'em up and stick them in a bunch of kiddie pools. It's not as cool as it sounds," Beckett explained offhandedly, as he got up and grabbed a bag of licorice that was on the island.

"How do you know?" Simon questioned, surprised. Was there something he was missing here? Some packet or booklet or handout he had missed? He looked around the table and checked the floor to be sure.

"We just do, okay? We hear things. From other kids. Funtastic Summer is not *fun*, okay Dad?" Ben said, shaking his head as he grabbed a piece of licorice.

"Well, then why is it called *Funtastic*?" Simon asked, forehead creased.

"I don't know, it's probably just their way of getting people's money or something," suggested Beckett with a shrug. He chewed on the end of a piece of licorice as he wobbled his chair back and forth.

Simon had to laugh, he loved the way kids thought. "Okay, so Funtastic Summer is out. What do you guys think? Have you heard anything about the other choices?" He looked back and forth between them, waiting for one of them to reply.

"Well, I know some kids in my class go to the one at the YMCA," offered Ben quietly, then added slowly, "but I don't really want to hang out with *them* all summer."

By *them*, Simon assumed Ben meant the boys who had been hard on him at the beginning of the school year. He frowned, thinking of what they had put Ben through. He considered no news good news on that front, and he hadn't heard anything since the incident months ago when they had made Ben cry. He was about to ask how things were going when Ben spoke up.

"They're not being mean again or anything, Dad. It's just that I don't feel good when I'm around them, so I'd really not like to be stuck with them all summer." Ben slouched in his chair, his eyes barely meeting Simon's.

Simon noticed Beckett laid his hand gently on Ben's shoulder, and tears sprung to his eyes. He was so thankful that Ben and Beckett had each other. He could see in Beckett Olive's kind heart and boundless loyalty. There was something in Beckett that put both Simon and Ben at ease, something strong and steady and reassuring. He had a way about him that calmed them, something that silently spoke to their hearts and gave them hope and a gentle strength that blew Simon away.

Sensing Simon's momentary inability to speak, Beckett piped up, "Plus, Tucker and his brother Colin are going to the one at school, remember? They were talking about it the other day on the bus!"

Ben's face lit up at the thought of spending more time with his neighborhood friend. "Let's do that one, Dad!" requested Ben. Then he gave Beckett a quick hug, followed by a soft bump on the arm, saying, "It's good you remembered, Beckett."

Simon squinted down at the handouts, "So which one is the one at school again?" he asked, shuffling through all the papers.

"Dad!" Both boys chorused.

"Ah, okay, here it is, Diary of an Awesome Summer. Looks like you boys better get out your pen and paper, because it's diary time!" Simon joked, laughing loudly.

"Really, Dad?" Beckett asked.

"Wow," Ben added a second later.

Simon just shrugged his shoulders at them as he got up to find a pen and start the process of filling out the registration for their chosen summer program.

Suddenly bored from all the sitting around, Ben stood up, pushing his chair back so quickly it crashed to the floor. "Bet you I can do a better flip on the tramp than you can!" he challenged Beckett, as he started to run out the door to the backyard.

"No way! Mine is way better than yours, just watch! Then we can do 1-2-3 tushie after the flip competition, okay?" Beckett called after Ben, skidding on the hardwood as he chased after his brother.

"Ben, get back here and pick up your chair!" Simon called after them. His answer was the loud slamming of the door. "Well, at least they remembered to shut it this time," he muttered to himself, slowly smiling.

Filling out the forms took longer than expected. Simon was confused when it had asked for grade level. Shouldn't the school already know what grades they were in? What was he supposed to put, their current grades or what they would be in after summer? He asked the boys, but there was no response.

Then there was the part where you had to decide what they would have for lunch each day. Would they have the school-packed lunch? Would they have lunch sent from home? If they had lunch from home, it had to be a nut-free lunch. Also it had to be completely disposable and preferably organic and gluten-free. He didn't know what half that stuff meant, so he decided to choose the school-packed lunch. To be nice he asked the boys if they minded. He was pretty sure they wouldn't answer; they hadn't before. He was wrong.

"Ew! No way, Dad! Those school-packed lunches are disgusting!" Ben hollered, pretending to gag as he jumped as high as he could on the trampoline.

"Yeah, the sandwiches are soggy, and they use old jelly and fake peanut butter stuff. Everybody knows that. We want lunch from home, Dad!" Beckett cried, laughing as Ben bounced him high.

Simon sighed and forced himself to check the lunches-from-home box on the form. He would bet his right hand that the Funtastic Summer program didn't care one nickel what the kids ate. He wondered what he had gotten himself into.

* * *

Michael led her to the big oak tree where a group of children were sitting underneath, playing duck, duck, grey duck. They stood side by side watching them for a while, and Olive recognized the boy she had found crying under this very tree not too long ago. He looked happy now though, laughing and running along with all of the others. Olive felt her heart brighten at the thought and noticed herself sparkle just a little more.

There was one young girl who clearly stood out as the leader, pointing out which child hadn't had a turn yet and suggesting one of them get picked next. She pulled faces to make the others laugh, and whenever she sat down after her turn, she gave the child on each side of her a big, tight hug.

"She gives them their joy back," Michael noted, full of love.

Olive smiled. "I can see that," she said, "Who is she?"

"It's who I've brought you here to see," he replied. Reaching over he put his hand on her shoulder giving her peace, at the same time as the young girl stood up, turned, and started walking towards them.

The closer she got, the harder Olive's heart started to beat. Olive had recognized her in an instant, the moment she had turned around Olive knew who she was, but she was too stunned to say anything.

"Hello, Mama," the young girl said, and Olive fell to her knees. "It's okay, Mama, don't cry," she said, sitting down next to Olive and putting her small hand on Olive's back, rubbing gently.

It was ironic, Olive thought, that on their first meeting, her daughter would be the one comforting her. It was the exact opposite of all that Olive had ever imagined.

Beckett hadn't even been one yet when Olive had found out she was pregnant with their third child. She and Simon had both been surprised, so tired from still getting up at night with Beckett that they hadn't even been thinking about birth control.

Olive had been convinced from the beginning that it was a girl. She'd had visions dancing in her mind of pink bows and frilly dresses and all things girl. She loved her boys, of course, but having a little girl would be the icing on the cake.

She'd been four months along when things had started to go wrong. It had been a Friday night. Olive had just tucked Ben in and snuck a peak at Beckett to make sure he was sleeping when she'd started to get painful cramps. Worried, she'd called the nurse line, and they'd assured her it was normal but to set up an appointment with her OB if they continued the next day.

Even with Simon's hopeful reassurance that everything would be fine, Olive still hadn't been able to let go of the deep feeling of dread in the pit of her stomach that something was terribly wrong. She'd slept in fits and starts, and when she'd woke up the next morning and gone to the bathroom, there had been blood in her underwear.

When she'd arrived at her OB's office an hour later, her worst fears were confirmed. There was no heartbeat; she'd had lost the baby. Devastated, Olive and Simon had left the office, confused and broken, the doctor's voice ringing in their ears, "Sometimes these things happen, and there's nothing you can do."

The loss of the baby had cut deep into both of their hearts, and there'd been times Olive hadn't been sure they would make it through, but they had, eventually. A few months later, when talking about the baby had started to become a little easier, Simon had suggested they think about giving the baby a name. He'd had read somewhere that it could help them heal, and so he'd carefully broached the subject with Olive.

They'd been sitting on their bed on a Sunday morning, the sun streaming in bright and sure through their bedroom window. Ben and Beckett had been watching cartoons in the loft across the hall, laughing loudly at Mickey Mouse, and Simon had hoped their attention would last long enough for him to talk with Olive.

When he'd suggested it, Olive had gone silent for a beat. Then when she'd started crying quietly, Simon had been worried he'd made a mistake. But then Olive took his hand in hers and held it against her heart. She'd told him that deep down she'd been sure the baby had been a girl, that she'd dreamed of her just last night, and her name had been Bella. She had been thinking all morning of a way to bring it up to Simon, but she hadn't been sure how, but now she didn't need to because he had done it for her.

That afternoon when Olive and the boys had been napping, Simon had left with a plan in mind. When he'd returned, Olive had been just sitting the boys down for their snack. "What's this?" she'd asked, as Simon had walked in with a bright red balloon filled with helium and a small oak sapling.

"It's for Bella," Simon had said quietly, "When the boys are done with their snack, we are going to plant the tree and send her the balloon." He'd cleared his throat and quickly wiped his eyes with the back of his sleeve, and though Olive hadn't known it was possible, she had fallen in love with him even more that day.

"Mama," Bella said, "Mama, look."

Wiping her eyes, Olive sat back on her heels and looked to where her daughter was pointing and gasped, her breath taken away. In front of her sat the big oak tree where the kids had been playing duck, duck, grey duck, but now she saw that it was no ordinary tree. It looked strikingly similar to the oak tree they had planted all those years ago, the only difference was that it was a lot bigger, and it had red balloons tied to the branches. She wondered why she hadn't seen them before.

Sometimes, she heard her daughter whisper, *we can't see things until we're ready.* "It's my tree, Mama," Bella explained, smiling up at Olive. "Thank you so much for my tree." She giggled and then, looking over at it, added, "And the balloons, I really like the balloons."

"You're welcome," Olive replied slowly and watched her daughter wave to some children who were running around the tree.

"I gotta go now, Mama," Bella said, giving Olive a tight hug that filled her with bright, bright love, "I'll see you again soon." She ran off to join in the game the other kids were playing around the tree.

Olive watched her go, then turned to Michael. "How ...?" she trailed off, not knowing how to put into words all the thoughts that were running through her mind.

"She's amazing, isn't she?" Michael asked, glowing, "She reminds me a lot of you." Michael put his hand on her shoulder and gave her peace. He knew all of her questions, and he showed her the answers with a joy that made Olive's heart feel so big that it hurt.

She saw how her losing Bella had a purpose, that even though they'd lost a sweet child on Earth, she saw how Heaven had gained a beautiful angel. She saw in flashes all the children Bella had helped and all the love she had given.

Michael showed her Bella's heart. He showed her the brightness of it and how it beat with pure compassion, and when Olive saw it, she felt laughter bubble up inside of her. "That is what she does, Olive. She brings joy and laughter to the ones who need it the most."

Michael showed her Ben and Beckett. He showed her how Bella liked to play with them in their dreams and how deep down they knew she was their sister. Michael gave her peace and showed her how Bella could heal her family, how she could see the cracks in their hearts, and how if she put her hands on just the right spot, they would glow and glitter and heal.

He showed her the power of Bella's love, and how ever since Bella had arrived, it had been shining down on Olive and Simon, on Ben and Beckett, and it still did. He showed her the love Bella had for her brothers, fierce and protective and hopeful.

Olive's tears started to flow again when she saw the love Bella had for Simon, and the phrase *Daddy's girl* flashed through her mind. She felt how much, for such a long time, Bella had longed to nestle into Simon's arm and have him read to her, snuggle with her.

Michael showed Olive Bella's love for her, and in it she could feel strength and kindness and understanding, and in that moment she knew that Bella had always been meant for greatness.

Olive's heart swelled, thinking of her daughter. "You're right, she is amazing," she agreed. "Where did all that love come from?" she wondered aloud.

Michael shimmered, "From Him and from you. When you love someone, it stays with them forever."

"Forever is a long time," Olive commented, looking around her at all of the beauty, feeling her heart lighten.

"Yes," Michael agreed, "It is."

12

———

THE FIRST WEEK OF SUMMER BREAK HAD BEEN A SUCCESS, AND SIMON was very pleased, with himself as well as the boys. He had worked out his work schedule, so that he could take Fridays off; the rest of the week the boys would be going to their Diary of an Awesome Summer program.

Mara offered again to take each of the boys for a week of one-on-one time. This was a tradition started when Ben was five, and it had been going on every summer since. This summer the boys countered, asking if they could go together to Gizzy's house for both of the weeks.

Simon wasn't surprised and neither was Mara. Ben and Beckett had grown closer since Olive's death and sometimes had a difficult time being away from each other more than a couple days. It was both a blessing and a curse in Simon's eyes, and something he knew they would eventually have to work on, but he was hoping it might resolve itself over time.

Olive had been gone now for close to ten months, and though things were getting easier, they were by no means back to how they had been before. Simon knew things probably would never go back to how they were before, and he was beginning to be okay with that, but still, he didn't want the boys to become so dependent on each other that it stunted their emotional growth. He wasn't too worried about it though. He was pretty sure they were going to be okay. It was just something he knew he should keep his eye on.

Ben and Beckett enjoyed their first week at summer camp. They went swimming at the local community pool, without funky fish, but they were okay with that. They started an ongoing tetherball competition with some of the other kids in their program.

Beckett came home one afternoon and tried to explain to Simon the rules of their new game and how you could get to be a 'king' of tetherball. Simon was so confused and asked so many questions that Beckett finally said, in an apologetic tone, "Oh, forget it, Dad. I guess you just weren't cut out for this type of sport."

One of the days it was raining on and off, so they watched a *Diary of a Wimpy Kid* movie. Once again Simon had no clue what they were talking about, so Ben made Simon promise that on Friday, after they ate at Saucy Baby, they would watch the first movie in the series. Apparently, there was more than one. Simon wasn't sure, he had seen his fair share of bad kids' movies, but Ben and Beckett promised him he would love it.

When Friday rolled around, Simon took the boys mini golfing, and then they went home where they played baseball, football, and basketball. After Ben and Beckett thoroughly whipped Simon's butt at a game of two-on-one, Simon limped inside where he went about chugging three huge glasses of water. Then he slowly made his way to the couch, lowering himself gingerly onto the cushions where he assessed just how out of shape he was. He looked out the back window where the boys and their friends were jumping heartily on the trampoline and wondered how they did it.

He hoped after the day was through that the boys would crash. He could do with an easy bedtime and maybe a long, hot bath. He laughed gamely at how pathetic he seemed, smiling at the happy shrieks of his kids outside.

After a couple of hours lounging around, trying to watch some baseball on TV, but mostly yelling at the kids who came running through his house like tornados to "shut the door!," he got up and called out to Ben and Beckett, letting them know they were going to leave to get dinner in half an hour. They were now scootering up and down the sidewalk, pretending to pick up invisible passengers while they fought bad guys from *Star Wars*.

Dragging himself up the stairs, he made his way into the shower and set the water to as hot as it could get. It burned his skin, and he winced at first, but it seemed to help his sore muscles. Then he dressed in jeans and an old gray t-shirt, feeling his heart pinch as he looked at Olive's side of the closet. He knew he had to go through it sooner than later, but his heart just wasn't in it yet. He would probably end up donating most of her stuff, but he couldn't stand the thought of another woman walking down the street with Olive's favorite sweatshirt on or going to sleep wearing the brand-new pajamas he'd bought her, the ones she'd never gotten a chance to wear. He wasn't ready, not yet.

Simon loaded the boys in the car, storing their scooters in the rack he and Olive had made last summer. There were memories of her all over the place, and sometimes the pain would still sneak up on him, stealing his breath away and making his heart break all over again. There had been times though, popping up more often, where her memory would make him smile. Make him laugh. Those times were almost more surprising than the painful ones because at no point before had he thought he'd ever make it to a place where remembering her would give him joy.

Something was shifting inside of him, and at first he had tried to stop it because he felt it wasn't right to be happy or laugh when she wasn't around. He was coming to see things differently now. There was a feeling inside of him, something deep down, that was telling him that this was what she would have wanted. For him to be happy. To laugh. To enjoy life.

Sometimes it seemed that was easier said than done. Just because he knew Olive would want him to enjoy life again didn't make it any easier for him to let her go and move on. There were still mornings when he'd open his eyes and the memory of her being gone was so devastating he could barely force himself out of bed. Thankfully he had Ben and Beckett; they were his motivation to keep going.

Things might have been getting easier, but they were still hard. He was trying though, as best he could in his own way, and even though there was a part of him that could never bear to let her go, there was another part of him, a bigger part, which was becoming hopeful of the future.

Not only had the boys talked him into watching *Diary of a Wimpy Kid* on Netflix, but they had also convinced him that a true movie night included Twizzlers and popcorn, with the special seasoning that Olive used to buy. They had none of these supplies—hence a trip to Target.

Pulling into the Target parking lot, Simon turned to his boys as he shut off the car, saying, "This movie better be good, guys, or next time I get to choose, and you know what that means."

Ben and Beckett groaned as they unhooked their seatbelts and got out of the car. Slamming his door, Ben looked appalled, declaring, "Come on, Dad, you have got to pick something other than *The Goonies* next time. I mean, it's a good movie, but we've seen it like a billion times."

"Don't worry, Ben, we both know our movie is *way* better," Beckett declared as he fell in step between his brother and his dad.

Simon shook his head, muttering, "Not possible."

Walking into the store, Simon led the way to the popcorn aisle and then stood back as Ben and Beckett scoured the shelves for their seasoning of choice. Simon wondered when he'd ever watch a movie that wasn't rated PG or G again.

Olive had loved watching movies. She was always adding more to their Netflix list, much to Simon's slight dismay. Sometimes the movies she picked were good, but a lot of them ended up being flops. Simon always joked that on the nights when Olive chose the movie, he knew to prepare himself for disappointment.

He really didn't much mind watching the movies Olive had chosen. It was kind of fun to see what was in store for them, what newly released movie Olive had found while browsing through Netflix. He sometimes even looked forward to it, way more than he would have admitted to Olive. Simon simply enjoyed spending time with her, snuggling on the couch with a bowl of popcorn or ice cream, depending on if Olive was craving sweet or salty that night.

He wasn't big on watching movies alone. Usually if he ended up turning on the TV, he would just flip through the channels until he found a sports game to watch. If there was nothing of interest on, he might go on Netflix and browse through the new TV series that had been added, maybe watching an episode or two.

But now, with Olive gone, he figured he was doomed to watch Disney movies or possibly unlimited amounts of Phineas and Ferb for the rest of his life. He wasn't sure he could stand it, and so for all of their sakes, he hoped the movie the boys were talking about was as good as they said it was.

"We found it, Dad! Here it is!" Beckett cried as they ran toward him down the aisle they'd been searching in.

Holding up the parmesan-garlic seasoning and a bag of popcorn, Ben remarked, "I'm so glad we found the movie on Netflix, I really didn't want to watch *The Goonies* again. Talk about torture."

Simon sighed as he grabbed the seasoning and popcorn. He thought about the picture of the movie they wanted to watch on Netflix, the one with an awkward boy on it. He sighed again. "This better be good, guys," he uttered doubtfully as they went in search of the Twizzlers, then walked to the checkout lane.

As they were waiting in line to pay, Beckett glanced over into the line next to them and cried out, "Ms. Thorne! Hi, Ms. Thorne!"

"Hi, Beckett," she replied, smiling over at them, "What are you guys up to?"

Simon smiled back, answering, "Just picking up some popcorn and Twizzlers for movie night." He held up the popcorn seasoning, shaking it a little and joked, "Lucky me."

"Thankfully we found our movie on Netflix. Otherwise it would be Dad's turn to choose what we watch and—yuck," Ben told her.

Ms. Thorne laughed, offering, "His choice couldn't be that bad, could it?"

"Um, yeah," Beckett piped up, "It could. *The Goonies*. Seen it *way* too many times."

"Okay, that is bad," Ms. Thorne agreed, making a face, "Once is enough for me."

Simon reddened as she sent him a quick wink, then shrugged, commenting, "What can I say, who wouldn't want to find buried treasure?"

Ms. Thorne laughed as Beckett asked, "Hey, we're going to Saucy Baby after this, do you want to come? We're going to play in the arcade, and Dad said I could get extra cheese on my pizza this time."

Shaking his head, Simon quickly replied, "Beckett, I'm sure Ms. Thorne has plans. It's going to be a boys' night, remember?"

"Come on, Dad. It's always boys' night," Ben quipped, looking glum.

Beckett nodded, sticking his lip out and begging, "Please, Dad?"

Simon looked down at his boys, not knowing what to say. He wouldn't mind if Ms. Thorne joined them, but he didn't want her to feel uncomfortable. He wasn't sure what the etiquette was for spending time with students and their families you worked with outside of school hours. Even though she had joined them once before at Saucy Baby, he was pretty sure that had been a special case, since Olive had just died and they were all struggling.

Before Simon could reply, Ms. Thorne cut in, "I don't have any plans tonight, actually. So if your dad is okay with it, I'd love to join you. Then I can challenge you both to a game of ski-ball." Looking over at Simon, she shrugged her shoulders as if to say, "Why not?"

Simon smiled, relieved. "That would be great, Ms. Thorne," he said above his boys' cheers.

"I'll see you there!" Ms. Thorne called out as her line moved up, and she unloaded her items onto the checkout belt.

Simon looked ahead at the slow-moving line they stood in and wondered why it seemed like he always chose the line that took twice as long as all the rest. Ignoring his boys excited shouts about beating Ms. Thorne at ski-ball, Simon silently called out to Olive for patience. Surprisingly their line sped up, and it was their turn to pay in no longer than one minute.

Pulling out his wallet, Simon glanced at the young checkout guy and smiled.

"Hey, little dudes!" the guy exclaimed, "Whoever picked out this popcorn seasoning has awesome taste. Let me guess, movie night?"

"It was us! We chose it!" Beckett answered proudly, then added, "We're watching *Diary of a Wimpy Kid* tonight!"

The checkout guy nodded enthusiastically as he scanned their purchases, saying, "Right on, dudes! Love that movie!"

Simon was still doubtful, questioning, "So you've seen it, and it's actually good?" Simon scanned his card, waiting for the guy to confess that he hadn't seen it but was just trying to be nice.

"Oh, yeah," the guy confirmed, clearing his throat, "I consider myself to be an expert on all things entertainment." He told them, standing up a little taller, obviously happy someone was asking his opinion, "And that movie is pretty darn funny. Enjoy!" He smiled, giving Ben and Beckett high-fives.

"Thanks," Simon replied, thinking the guy probably had no idea what he was talking about. Simon could feel a headache starting to form behind his eyes, which always happened when he hadn't eaten much during the day. He tried to remember what he'd had for lunch but couldn't think of anything. Then he remembered that he'd made the boys lunch but had been too exhausted to find something for himself.

"See," Ben said laughing, as they walked out of the store towards their car, "He's an expert and he says it's good, so you know it will be!"

"Yeah, Dad!" Beckett chimed in, bouncing beside them, happily swinging their bag of purchases.

Ben frowned, pondering, "I wonder how he became an expert?" His forehead creased as he thought about it, wondering how he could become one too.

"How can he be an expert, Dad?" Beckett questioned as they got into their car, "Dad? Dad! What's 'expert,' Dad? What's 'en-ter-tain-ment,' Dad? Dad! *Daaddd*!!!"

Simon clenched his jaw, thinking how Beckett sometimes had a little too much energy for him. "Let's just get to Saucy Baby, and we can talk about it there, okay? I'm starving."

"And crabby," Beckett noted.

Simon shot him a look as they backed out of the parking spot.

Ben turned away, pretending to look out the window as they pulled out of the parking lot, quietly laughing to himself. Today had been a good day. He felt happy, and he liked that he knew that was okay. *Love you Mom*, he thought and smiled softly.

13

Jo Thorne pulled into the parking lot of Saucy Baby and slowly searched for an empty spot. It was a Friday night and the pace was packed, as usual. Friday nights meant that Lucy would be working the pizza oven, and that meant the best pizza of the week.

Jo had been coming to Saucy Baby for as long as she could remember. In her opinion it was the only place to go if you wanted a decent slice of pizza. Because Saucy Baby was her favorite restaurant, Jo made a point to get to know the staff and had been surprised when, a couple years ago, she had stopped in and seen a new face at the pizza oven. Jo knew the owner, Benno, was incredibly particular about who he allowed to run the oven, not wanting to compromise their reputation of what he called 'pizza perfection.'

Jo had waved a quick hello at the girl, red faced-from the heat of the oven, and then walked to where Benno was standing at the back of the restaurant. "Who's the new girl?" she'd questioned, surprised.

"That's Lucy, and she's amazing." Benno told her, glancing over at Lucy and giving her a thumbs-up, "A natural, ultimate pizza perfection going on over there." He winked at Jo, then asked, "Want your usual?"'

Jo had nodded and when she'd gotten her usual of pepperoni with extra cheese, she had been pleasantly surprised. Jo had to agree, the girl had skills.

Since then Saucy Baby had been written up in many food articles, blogs, and magazines for their amazing pizza and great service. Lucy had gotten married, and Benno, worried she would leave Saucy Baby in the dust, had offered her a raise and let her set her own schedule. Hence the reason for the especially packed parking lot on Friday nights.

Finally spotting a parking spot at the very back of the lot, Jo pulled in and smiled, thinking of Beckett, Ben, and Simon.

It was true that she rarely met up and had dinner with kids she worked with and their parents. She sometimes got invited to their homes to eat and talk about what was going on at school or at home, with both children and parents, but that felt more like business because it involved work.

She thought back to the last time she had met Simon and the boys at Saucy Baby and how she had agreed because they had all looked so sad, so she had wanted to be there for them. Both Ben and Beckett had been having a hard time getting back into their regular routine after Olive died, and she had hoped that spending time with them outside of school might help her connect with them. She had wanted them to know that they could talk to her about anything and that she was there for them. It was important to her that they knew there was someone at school that was looking out for them.

She had met them out that first time because of work, but this time, well, she felt she had agreed more out of pleasure than business. She honestly enjoyed Ben and Beckett. They were both good kids who more and more lately had smiles on their faces whenever she saw them. The only way she could explain how she felt when she saw them happy was that it made her own heart happy. She hadn't ever felt this much love towards any of the other children she had worked with before, but she was certain it was because she had known their mother and had seen firsthand how losing a parent could completely devastate a child. Her heart broke for them, and it meant so much to her to see them heal.

She thought about Simon. She had a soft spot in her heart for him as well. Jo remembered how he had struggled to find his own way and figure out what was right for his boys. He had floundered for a long time before she had seen a confidence bloom up inside of him, and somehow that made her care even more.

To see him struggle and be so open about it, to see him not be afraid of being vulnerable was beautiful to Jo. She had seen her fair share of parents who would hide their feelings from the children, thinking it was better to show no emotion at all. Jo could see those children watching their parents, learning from them, and so many times she had wanted to beg and plead with the parents to be honest. Implore them to teach their children that showing emotions was good because if you just hid them away, how would you ever learn how to deal with them?

She was proud of Simon for not being afraid to show his boys that it was okay to feel all that they were feeling, that it was normal. She knew it hadn't been easy for him, probably still wasn't, but they were making progress, and that was what mattered most.

Jo grabbed her purse and slammed her car door shut, hitting the lock button on her key fob twice to hear the chirp. Glancing over her shoulder, she saw Simon, Ben, and Beckett walking towards the entrance. "Hiya boys!" Jo called out, as she quickened her pace to catch up to them.

Simon slowed down and grabbed Beckett's hand to stop him from bouncing off the sidewalk and headfirst into a truck that had pulled into the lot.

"Hi, Ms. Thorne," the three of them chorused.

When Jo caught up to them, she gave both boys high-fives and laughed when she saw the expression on Simon's face. "Long day?" she asked smiling down at the boys.

Simon sighed dramatically for effect and pulled open the heavy door, confirming, "I'm exhausted, and we still have a movie to watch after this."

"That bad, huh?" Jo asked. Nudging Ben, she said in a stage whisper, "I think your dad's about to pass out. What did you guys do to him?"

Ben looked at his dad and rolled his eyes, then as they walked into Saucy Baby, he spotted Lucy and waved, asking, "Can we go say hi, Dad?

"Yeah, please, Dad!" Beckett begged, bouncing up and down and waving his hands in front of Simon's face.

Simon gave his boys a nudge and off they ran to say hello. He glanced over at Jo, who had turned her face, so he wouldn't see her laughing. "Laugh all you want," he said, rubbing this sore neck (he must have pulled a muscle while playing basketball, or maybe when falling asleep on the couch?), then added half joking, "You wouldn't understand."

Jo raised her eyebrows and gave him a skeptical look. "Oh yeah, try me," she challenged.

Just then Ben and Beckett ran back, excited expressions on their faces.

"Dad!" Beckett cried, grabbing Simon's hand, pulling him towards the back of the restaurant where the arcade was. "Dad! Lucy said someone will come get us when our table is ready, so let's go play ski-ball!"

"It won't be for like 20 minutes or something, so we can play in the arcade until then, okay, Dad!" Ben shouted as he ran for his favorite pinball game.

Simon lurched forward as Beckett tugged his hand insistently. Simon groaned, his visions of relaxing in a quiet booth evaporating. "Do all kids have this much energy, or is it just mine?"

"This," Jo chuckled, winking at Beckett, "is nothing. Come to school with me one day, and you'll be amazed."

"I think I'll pass," Simon replied, paling a little as he handed Beckett two quarters for the ski-ball machine.

If Jo was being honest about seeing kids with even more energy than his, then he wasn't sure how she did it. Simon glanced over to his left, where Ben and Jo were high-fiving each other at the pinball machine. He felt something shift and lighten in his heart, and he realized it was happiness. Jo looked over at him and smiled, a dimple flashing quickly, and Simon felt his heart skip a beat. He smiled back and turned his attention to Beckett, confused at the fluttering in his chest.

Telling himself it was nothing, that he was just happy to be enjoying time with another adult, Simon grabbed the ball and tossed it, aiming for the 100 slot.

He felt confused and guilty because he was lying to himself and he knew it. The last time he had felt this fluttering in his chest like he did now was when he had first met Olive. Olive hadn't even been gone a year, and already he was having feelings for another woman. Simon was ashamed. He wondered what Olive would think.

* * *

Olive felt like she'd been stabbed in the heart, and for a moment she couldn't breathe. She felt like she was going to die and wondered if it were possible for her to be dying a second, more painful death.

"What's going on?" she asked, as she felt Michael's presence beside her. Michael touched her shoulder and an image flashed before Olive. An image of Simon and Ben and Beckett playing games in an arcade. There was a woman there with them, high-fiving Ben and smiling at Simon.

Olive turned her eyes to Simon. She noticed the way he looked at the woman, could feel his heartbeat speed up in his chest. She saw the surprise and guilt flash in his eyes, and she knew something big was happening.

He's falling in love, she thought simply, and the words hit her like a dagger in the heart. Tears falling, she turned to Michael, "I'm right, aren't I?"—she wept—"He's falling in love with her."

Michael nodded slowly and held a hand to her heart. Olive felt the pain gradually ease away, leaving only a small ache in its place.

Michael didn't say anything as he gently pulled his hand away, but he didn't need to. Olive could hear his thoughts echoing inside of her head. "I know this was what I wanted, for him to find love again," she sniffed, "but why does it have to hurt so much?"

"You love him, Olive. For so long you've loved him. It's not an easy thing to see someone you've loved so much fall in love with someone else," Michael said simply.

Olive shook her head. "But I let him go!" she cried, "I told him I wanted him to do this! I thought letting go would mean I wouldn't feel like this anymore." She sobbed.

Michael took her hand, he gave her peace. "Yes, you let him go," he affirmed, "but you still love him, you always will. It takes time to understand, time to get to a place where you can see that no matter what happens, everything's going to be okay."

"I just don't want to lose him," she whispered, letting go of his hand to wipe her eyes.

Michael shimmered, and Olive looked closely at him, wondering what he was going to say. "There will come a time when you'll realize that there is no loss. That what looks like loss now is really just a new beginning."

"Really?" Olive asked hopefully, eyebrows knit together, unsure. Even though she'd gone through an amazing transformation, she still sometimes felt like a yo-yo, her emotions ranging from high highs to low lows. She might be an angel, but right now she sure didn't feel like one.

Some things take time, she heard him whisper.

Michael smiled, grew bright, explaining, "You'll look around and all you'll see is love, love everywhere, and hope, and it will be a beautiful thing."

Noticing Olive's uncertainty, Michael reached his hand out towards her. "Here," he said, "take my hand. I'll show you what I see."

"Will it hurt?" Olive asked, slowly placing her palm in his.

"Only a little," he promised, and closing his fingers around hers, he eased her in gently.

"Open your eyes," he whispered.

Olive could feel it pressing in on her, beating a rhythm against her heart like the bass drums in a marching band. It made her heart ache in the way that it did when she thought of how much she loved her boys, only it was bigger. It hurt, but it wasn't bad. It was just so much good that it was hard to take in. Olive shook her head. "I don't think I can," she confessed.

"Open your eyes," Michael said again, and Olive could feel him around her, buffering her from the intensity.

Slowly, slowly, Olive opened her eyes, and what she saw took her breath away. Michael was right, there was so much beauty here, so much love. It was everywhere she looked, in every action she saw, and before she knew it, tears were running down her cheeks.

This love was big and bright and true, and she could *see* it! Flowing out from the trees, the grass, the sun. Rushing along with the rivers and lakes and oceans, bursting out of each and every flower. Radiating out of every person on the planet. She noticed the brightness of the love flowing out of children. She turned to Michael, questioning.

It's so much easier for them to love freely, he explained, sparkling.

Olive thought of her family and saw them immediately. She saw her boys, the brilliance of their love all around them. She saw Simon and his tender heart, beating stronger, slowly healing, getting brighter. It was all too much to take in, so she closed her eyes.

When she opened them again, everything was gone.

Olive smiled up at Michael. "Thank you," she said.

He shimmered.

Olive thought again of her family, of Simon loving someone else. It still hurt, but not as much, and she realized she hadn't seen the woman's face. "Who was it, with Simon and the boys?" she asked Michael, her voice cracking. "Who's he falling for?" The words pained her, but she knew it was what she wanted—for Simon to find someone he and the boys could love, someone who could love them back.

"Jo," Michael answered, sending with it love and understanding.

Olive had never before felt how heavy the weight of a single word could be until now, never before realized how much meaning two simple letters strung together could hold for her. It had been hard to let Simon go, even harder now when she realized that someone else might be taking her place. But she could see how they fit together, saw when the four of them combined, the wonderful life they could have.

She wanted that so much for them, wanted them to be happy and live a good life, filled with love. Surprisingly, the wanting of that happiness for them made the hurt in her heart disappear, and Olive laughed through her tears. "Yes," she agreed, feeling her broken heart slowly piece back together. "Yes," she said again, nodding, "She's perfect."

* * *

In Simon's dream they were sitting in the backyard on the porch swing, holding hands and watching the sunset.

"I love you," she said to him, smiling brightly.

Her smile and the light in her eyes lit up his heart, and he knew she meant it. "I love you, too," he replied, holding onto her hand more tightly. She was slipping away, he could feel it, but he wasn't ready to let her go quite yet.

"It's okay," she added, "to love her." She looked into his eyes and squeezed his hand, sending him peace.

"To love who?" Simon asked, his heartbeat speeding up a notch.

"Jo," Olive replied easily. Letting go of the last remnants of pain, she watched them fall to the ground and disappear.

Simon saw it too. "What was that?" he asked, surprised.

"My pain," Olive replied. "It's gone now. You can let yours go too."

Simon shook his head. "I'm not sure I can," he admitted. "I love you too much."

"Sometimes loving someone is letting them go," Olive explained, then added softly, "It's okay, Simon. I promise."

Olive shimmered before his eyes, and he felt the love she was sending him and knew what she said was true.

"I don't know how," he whispered, swallowing loudly.

"Here," Olive said, holding out her other hand, "let me help you."

Simon turned towards her and grabbed her hand, amazed at her strength.

"You're strong too, Simon. Stronger than you know," remarked Olive, holding both his hands in hers.

Simon blinked, stunned. "How did you know what I was thinking?"

Olive laughed, confiding, "It's one of the perks of being an angel."

Simon smiled slowly at her, feeling peace fill his heart. "I should be more surprised than I am, but I'm not." He took in her bright glow and laughed, adding, "I guess it just makes sense."

Olive shimmered. "Ready?" she asked.

"Ready as I'll ever be," Simon said, looking into her eyes.

Olive smiled and sparkled. She gave him peace and courage. "Close your eyes," she said, "and I'll show you."

Simon closed his eyes, and Olive showed him many things. She showed him her love for him and the boys. She showed him their daughter and all of her beauty. She showed him who she was now and who she hoped to become. Lastly, she showed him her heart, and in it he saw the truth and knew it was okay for him to move on and be happy because it was what she wanted the most, for him and their boys.

And so he let go. He opened up his heart and let the light shine in on all of the dark spaces until there was nothing left but hope and love and happiness.

"Open your eyes," Olive said.

Slowly Simon opened his eyes, and when he did, he saw all of his pain fall away, drifting down to the spot where Olive's had disappeared a moment ago.

"Olive," he said, turning to thank her, but when he looked over, she had her finger to her lips.

"Shh, look," she instructed, pointing to the spot where their pain had fallen.

Flowers were growing and sprouting one after another before his very eyes, and he was surprised to feel tears running down his cheeks.

"How is that happening?" he asked, his throat tight with emotion.

Olive shimmered so brightly that Simon had to close his eyes. "Love," Olive replied and laughed softly, dimming her shine.

"Love?" Simon asked, opening his eyes once again. "But I thought it was our pain."

"It is," Olive said simply, "it's both. It's pain transformed into something new. It's love and new beginnings." Olive slowly released her grip on Simon's hands and sat back.

Simon felt Olive slipping away again, but he wasn't ready, he wanted more time with her. "Olive, please, don't go," Simon pleaded, "not yet."

Olive smiled at Simon. She gave him peace and love and courage, saying, "Thank you for being so good to me, Simon. Thank you for loving me like you did. You made my life beautiful, and I couldn't ask for more."

Simon felt more tears coming, and he wiped them away with the tips of his fingers. He told her, "I'm so sorry, Olive. About your accident. I wish I could have done something to save you."

"Don't be," Olive answered. "It wasn't your fault, and you know that."

"I know," Simon said, nodding. "I love you, Olive. I don't think I'll ever find anyone that I can love as much as I loved you."

Olive shimmered, prompting, "I know, but I want you to try. You know that too."

Simon smiled, confirming, "You're right, I do. Thanks to you. You've done an amazing job at helping us all heal." He laughed, musing, "Sometimes I can't believe it's actually real."

Olive laughed too, and Simon thought he heard bells chiming.

"So, since you're an angel now, does that mean you'll watch out for us? Make sure we're safe?" Simon asked half joking.

"Always," Olive promised, smiling softly at him.

"It's time, isn't it?" Simon asked, feeling Olive slowly pulling away.

"It is," Olive said easily. "Goodbye, Simon. I'll always love you." Olive leaned forward and kissed him on the cheek and was gone.

"Goodbye, Olive. I'll always love you too," Simon replied as he watched her go.

* * *

Simon woke with a start and looked around the room, realizing the dream he'd been having wasn't just a normal dream. Olive had been to visit him, but it was different than the last time. Where it had been blurry and out of focus then, it had been crystal clear, live, and in technicolor this time. He sat up and took stock of his heart. It didn't feel as heavy as it had for the past year; in fact, it felt lighter than he could remember it feeling in a long, long time.

Sure, there was still sorrow around the edges, but it was more bittersweet than painful. Mostly though, there was just light—pure, bright, unconditional light.

Simon thought about his life going forward. About Ben and Beckett, about Jo. He knew it was time to take the next step, but he wasn't quite sure what that was.

"What happens next?" he wondered aloud to himself.

That, he could have sworn he heard Olive whisper, *is entirely up to you.*

* * *

What Mara liked best about Jo, second to the fact that she loved Simon and the boys unconditionally, as if they'd always been hers, was that there was no awkwardness when it came to Olive. There were no uncomfortable silences or tense moments, only openness and love and laughter.

Mara noticed right away how Jo made a point to keep Olive's memory alive. She noticed how Jo would sit next to Ben and Beckett, as if she had all the time in the world to listen to their memories of their mother. How when Mother's Day and Olive's birthday rolled around, Jo helped the boys and Simon celebrate by releasing colorful balloons and planting Olive's favorite flowers beside the porch swing.

She knew when to step back and give Simon his space, and when to give him that extra nudge that he needed to keep moving on.

There was never a time when Jo didn't approve of or encourage talk about Olive. Mara knew it couldn't be easy, living in someone else's shadow, taking someone else's place, but there was something about Jo that made it look effortless.

"It is," Jo replied when Mara complimented her on her approach. Mara wanted to thank Jo, let her know how much it meant that her boys had someone like her in their lives.

"Simon, Ben, and Beckett, they mean the world to me. I love them so much that it *is* effortless. It would be a lot harder for me not to spend my life with them," confided Jo to Mara. Jo was touched that she had been accepted so completely by this loving family. "I have a deep respect for Olive, and all that she did for her family. I guess I don't see me as much taking someone's place, I more see me stepping in and doing what I can do for them. As much as I wish I could be the person she was to them, I'm not Olive and I never will be. But I know who I am, and I know that I will do my best by them as long as I'm can," Jo went on to say, then paused, looking thoughtful, and added softly, "It means a lot to me that you approve. My hope is that Olive would too."

Just then a huge stack of napkins blew off the kitchen island and flew around and around, gently landing scattered on the kitchen table. Mara smiled to herself as Jo wondered aloud where the open window was.

Realizing the boys hadn't yet told Jo the special way Olive made her presence known, Mara stepped forward, pulling Jo into a tight hug. "Yes," she said, through happy tears, "I'm pretty sure she would."

14

THERE WERE MORE BALLOONS ON THE OAK TREE, NOT JUST RED, BUT ALL different colors. Something tugged at Olive's heart as she looked at them, she knew they were special, but why?

Aren't they pretty, Mama? Bella asked, in her sweet voice.

Yes, they are, Olive replied. *Who are they for?*

They're for you, Mama, Bella said simply, *can't you feel in your heart they're for you?*

Yes, she said, *but why? Who are they from?*

Close your eyes, Mama. Feel with your heart, Bella instructed, as she placed her hand on Olive's chest, *They're from Daddy and Ben and Beckett. It's your birthday, Mama. Happy birthday!*

Olive closed her eyes and felt Bella showing her how to open her heart. *It's easier at first if you close your eyes, Mama. You won't have to all the time, but just try it to start. Just relax and open your heart like this. It's okay, Mama, it won't hurt.*

Following Bella's lead, Olive relaxed and slowly opened her heart. At first she felt sadness and tried to pull back, not wanting to let it in.

She felt Bella shake her head. *Stay open, Mama,* she whispered, *the happy comes next.*

Olive felt Bella giving her strength. She took it in and relaxed, opening her heart as big as she could. She felt the sadness again, but she stayed open, and what came next took her breath away.

She could feel Simon and Ben and Beckett, she could feel their joy and happiness, hear their laughter.

"We love you, Mom!" she heard Ben shout.

"Happy birthday, Mom!" they cried.

"I love you SO much, Mommy!" Beckett giggled.

"I love you, Olive," she heard Simon whisper.

It came in a rush and was gone, bittersweet, but oh-so beautiful.

You did it, Mama! You did it! Bella cried happily.

Olive opened her eyes and looked at Bella, her rosy cheeks glowing brightly. *I love you, Bella*, she said, *thank you for showing me how.*

You're welcome, Bella replied, *Now that you know how, you can do it whenever you want to. You just have to remember to let the hurt through first because if you close up before it's gone, you'll never get to the good stuff. Okay, Mama? Don't forget.*

Olive marveled at Bella. She marveled at her knowledge and her innocence, at the simple way she could show you what mattered most. She marveled at Bella's capacity to love and give joy to anyone who needed it. She marveled at her strength. *I won't forget*, she promised, as Bella ran off to play with her friends.

You know, Olive, all of those qualities that Bella has are in you too. They are in everyone. You just need to remember who you really are, and they're yours, Michael communicated with a smile. He shimmered and shined and sparkled.

Olive looked down at herself and smiled. She saw herself shimmering and shining and sparkling. For the first time in a long time she saw who she truly was. She saw who she used to be and who she was becoming. She saw that everything she had always wanted to be she already was, she realized she always had been.

She saw that she wanted to do great things, and she believed that she could. That she would. This was her purpose, her plan. This was her past and present and future. This was her now.

At this realization she grew brighter, brighter than she had ever been. She heard Bella laugh joyfully.

What's next? she asked, smiling at Michael.

Come, he said. *Let me show you the way.*

* * *

There were times when Olive went back. When her boys graduated high school and college. When they each, in turn, got married.

When Ben wrote a book about dyslexia that became the go-to book for parents and schools alike, and was used to educate teachers across the country—she was there with him, cheering him on with each word he wrote.

The first time Beckett spoke to children and their parents about what it was like to lose his mother, she was there in the audience, listening along with everybody else. She almost burst with love when he made the decision to become a motivational speaker, helping families deal with loss in the most positive ways.

When their babies were born and her boys became fathers, she was there. She wouldn't have missed it for the world. She liked to visit her grandchildren, tell them stories, and make them laugh. But only once in a while because she knew it would be too hard to go back.

Besides, she had things to do. Her mother was arriving tomorrow, and she wanted to be there to greet her.

* * *

"I love you, and I'm so proud of all that you've done. You're amazing," He said simply.

Olive felt His profound love and smiled. "Thank you. You probably say that to all of the people," she shimmered.

"Yes," He confirmed with a chuckle, "I do. But it's true."

"I know," she replied.

They stayed there for a while, sparkling in the night sky, while two boys sat on the roof of an old house, thinking about life.

"Those two stars are so bright," one boy said, pointing up towards the sky. "I sometimes wonder what makes some brighter than others."

The other laughed and replied, "It's probably Mom."

The first laughed too, agreeing, "It probably is," and then called out, "Hi, Mom!"

"We love you, Mom!" called out the other.

It was quiet for a while until one asked, "Can you believe it's been *30 years*?"

"No," the other replied, "it seems like just yesterday."

It was quiet again as they sat there together, silently remembering their mother.

Acknowledgements

FIRST, I WOULD LIKE TO THANK MY FAMILY – J, K, R, AND B – THIS BOOK is for you. You inspire me everyday to see the best in others and to view the world in a new way.

Thank you to my parents, Kathy and Terry, and also my brothers, Jon and Chris, for your support and great ideas.

To my pre-readers – Scott and Chris– thank you for your time and feedback, it means so much to me.

To Jenny H, an amazing photographer- thank you for a fun photo session which ended in talking over Italian sodas about dream jobs and new book ideas. You are so much fun!

Thank you to my editor, Nancy, who understands my writing style, and always corrects my run-on sentences.

Thank you to Ryan, at Mayfly Design, who came up with the most amazing cover designs for this book.

Thank you to my publicist, Rachel at RMA Publicity, for spreading the word about my book.

To my friends, family, book club crew and everyone else who has encouraged me along the way – thank you, thank you, thank you! Your support, curiosity, interest and excitement mean more to me than you will ever know.

Lastly, to anyone who might be going through a difficult time, please remember that you are never, truly alone. Whether you have lost someone you love, have a child struggling in school, or something else entirely, there is always someone out there who will understand you, see you, accept you and hear you. So, don't give up, keep going. I believe in you!

CPSIA information can be obtained
at www.ICGtesting.com
Printed in the USA
LVHW09s1702200918
590798LV00002B/280/P